"Just cancel it. I'll make it up to the kid getting the award. She could come for a tour of the company. I'll take her for lunch, or something."

Molly thought of Liam's jam-packed schedule. Where was she going to fit that in? She could feel a little headache gathering between her eyes, right over the bridge of her nose.

"How about if I go with you?" she said, impulsively.

She reminded herself she was not impulsive. There was always a price to be paid for being impulsive.

"Like pretend to be my date?" he asked, astonished.

"No, no, nothing like that!" She was blushing wildly.

"Oh," he said, snapping his fingers. "Like my plus-one."

Molly was aware her intent in offering her services for the evening had not been completely pure. It wasn't about finding a lunch slot in a tight schedule. And it wasn't just about being helpful in a new way, either.

No, she wanted to spend more time with him.

She was being greedy for his company, pure and simple.

And she, of all people, should know all about the dangers involved in wanting *more*.

Dear Reader,

This is a story of two worlds colliding. Despite running as far and as fast as she can, Molly's hard-scrabble beginnings are never as much behind her as she would like for them to be.

And Liam, successful in his own right, but born to wealth and privilege beyond imagining, has given up on anyone ever caring about him for *who* he is, not for *what* he has.

Against the backdrop of two of the world's most spectacular cities, New York and Quebec City, I invite you to travel with me as this intriguing couple overcomes all obstacles, to discover in each other answers to the longings common to all of us:

Someone to feel safe with;

Someone who loves you as you are;

Someone who will hold sacred your deepest secrets;

Someone to laugh with;

And, most of all, that very special someone who leads you to your heart's strongest yearning:

That place called home.

With best wishes,

Cara Colter

THE CEO'S PLUS-ONE CHARADE

CARA COLTER

Recycling programs for this product may not exist in your area.

ISBN-13: 978-1-335-47071-3

The CEO's Plus-One Charade

For questions and comments about the quality of this book, please contact us at CustomerService@Harlequin.com.

Harlequin Enterprises ULC
22 Adelaide St. West, 41st Floor
Toronto, Ontario M5H 4E3, Canada
www.Harlequin.com

HarperCollins Publishers
Macken House, 39/40 Mayor Street Uppe
Dublin 1, D01 C9W8, Ireland
www.HarperCollins.com

Printed in U.S.A.

Cara Colter shares her home in beautiful British Columbia, Canada, with her husband of more than thirty years, an ancient crabby cat and several horses. She has three grown children and two grandsons.

Books by Cara Colter

Harlequin Romance

A White Christmas in Whistler

The Billionaire's Festive Reunion

Blossom and Bliss Weddings

Second Chance Hawaiian Honeymoon
Hawaiian Nights with the Best Man

Fairy Tales in Maine

Invitation to His Billion-Dollar Ball

Summer Escapes

Cinderella's Greek Island Temptation

Winter Escapes

Their Hawaiian Marriage Reunion

Winning Over the Brooding Billionaire
Accidentally Engaged to the Billionaire
The Prince from Her Past

Visit the Author Profile page at Harlequin.com for more titles.

Dedicated to all those people working quietly in the background: the bank tellers; the store clerks; the custodians; the hair stylists; the teacher's aides; the secretaries. You make the world work. I'm grateful.

CHAPTER ONE

"How dare you?"

Molly Littleton held the phone away from her ear as insults rained down on her. This was the side of Eva La Lydia people did not see, she mused. Who knew the husky-toned actress could be quite so, well, shrill?

She waited patiently for a break in the rant, and then said, calmly, "I'm sorry, Miss La Lydia, but the nondisclosure agreement is not negotiable."

"How dare you insinuate I would kiss and tell?"

Molly closed her eyes. It was very tempting to remind the up-and-coming actress that she had done exactly that—kissed and told—on her last three boyfriends. Poor Douglas Hampton. The whole world now knew his kiss was garlic-tinged, rated *ewww*, by the actress.

Not that Molly's boss, Liam Westerhouse, would *ever* have garlic-tinged breath. And Molly was absolutely certain a kiss from him would also never be rated *ewww*.

Even though she was all alone in her office, thinking of Liam's kisses made her face suddenly feel hot, as if just by having the thought, she'd been caught in a terribly inappropriate situation.

She opened her eyes, bit her tongue and forced her thoughts in a different direction. As she often did under stress, she glanced around her office, taking in the order and subtle high-end touches with an inward sigh of deep delight.

Her neat desk had the soft, rich glow of solid walnut. The deep, luxurious pile of the wall-to-wall cream-colored wool rug absorbed sound, making her office a sanctuary of quiet in the middle of the world's busiest city. Two iconic black-and-white photos—the originals—were on the wall her desk faced, and depicted the very skyline she could look out on every single day.

She swiveled to those views now, and felt a sigh—arrival—within her. Not something that should be risked by giving into the temptation to give Miss La Lydia a piece of her mind. Or worse, allowing renegade thoughts of her boss's kisses.

The daylight was leaching from the New York skyline, being replaced by the office lights within the Manhattan office buildings popping on, one by one.

Molly still had to pinch herself about how far she had come from a rundown bayou neighborhood—closest big center, Shreveport, Louisiana—to *this*.

Still, evening falling was an urgent reminder of the task at hand and the fact time had run out. There was no way an NDA from Miss La Lydia could reach Molly's desk before the awards event,

Innovators on the Move, which was starting in two hours.

She was aware of feeling relieved. Who wanted to expose Liam to *that* for an entire evening?

"Perhaps we can work together another time," Molly lied smoothly.

Her suggestion was met with momentary—and blessed—silence, before the screeching ensued, worse than before.

"I'm nearly ready to go," the actress cried. "I'm being dressed by—" She named one of the best fashion houses in New York.

"I'm really sorry, Miss La Lydia, but without the NDA, we cannot possibly move forward."

She hoped that didn't mean Eva would offer to rush it over. Thankfully, that didn't happen.

"I'll have your job, you rude little snip," Molly heard as she was disconnecting. "I'll be calling Liam personally—"

Note to self, Molly thought, do not trust Francis, from publicity, to come up with red-carpet companion suggestions for their boss again, no matter how much good press and attention for the company and the event that they might generate.

She'd been trying to get that signed NDA agreement for weeks. She should have suspected something was up as the litany of excuses from Eva's assistant had piled up: could you send another copy; it was on its way; in the works; just needed a signature; lost by the building concierge.

Now, Molly was in the rarest of positions: caught

out. Her boss would be attending the publicity-generating awards show without a date. It wasn't the end of the world, but it also wasn't how her world worked. She glanced again at night falling on the city, and considered. Who could she ask to step in for La Lydia? Who on earth could be ready for a red-carpet event on such short notice?

She was just scrolling through her business phone when the door to the outer office was flung open and her boss strode in, all energy and confidence, and she felt that familiar sense of a world on snooze coming vibrantly to life, black and white turning to color.

Liam Westerhouse was gorgeous.

Stunningly, unforgettably, amazingly gorgeous.

Today, he was wearing a beautifully tailored suit, light gray jacket, with a crisp white shirt underneath it, knife-creased, narrow-legged slacks. Liam had a gift for always getting the tie exactly right and today it was exquisite—silk that held the multiple shades of the grays of storm clouds. Gold cufflinks winked at his wrists.

The suit subtly accentuated a beautiful build, slender rather than beefy.

And yet there was no mistaking the power in those shoulders, and in the length of his legs. His belly was flat beneath the shirt, his hips narrow.

And as compelling as all that was, it was his face that absolutely took her breath away. He had a mop of golden hair that never failed to look faintly messy, delightfully at odds with the perfectly put-together look of the suit.

That mane of luscious hair framed a face that was chiseled and flawless, with high cheekbones, strong nose, a faintly clefted chin. His chin and cheeks were roguishly whisker-shadowed. Like his untamed hair, the whiskers were an intriguing contrast, as if a secret outlaw wore the suit as a disguise.

But it was Liam's eyes that were his most stunning feature. Well, besides his generous mouth and the intriguing puffiness of his lower lip, which, given her renegade thoughts of earlier, she was simply not allowing herself to look at.

But his eyes! Framed in a fringe of sooty lashes, they might be called hazel, though that word really didn't do justice to the blend of green and gold and brown.

There was always something in them: a spark, a quality of dancing mischief that made her want to smile.

Even now, when she was aware she had let him down.

Before she made the admission of her failure, he stopped, cocked his head and looked at her. Really looked at her, in a way that made her feel seen.

Not, admittedly, that there was much to see. The designer suit—matching jacket and pencil skirt—that Molly had snagged at a high-end thrift store was a nice shade of cream that she hoped blended her in nicely with the carpet. She had left off the splurge item: a brand-new colorful silk scarf.

The scarf didn't go with her plan to notch down her appearance in direct correlation to her growing awareness that she had developed an embarrassing crush on her boss.

Some women might have amped up, but Molly was not that woman. It would just make her whole humiliating awareness of him all too obvious. It could make for awkwardness in the office.

Her office, run to her standards, was a very, very long way from the mail room where she had begun at Liam Westerhouse's company, FIX.

So, disruptions of a personal nature would simply not be tolerated.

Today, Molly had made herself particularly invisible. As well as choosing a beautifully cut but otherwise bland suit (from her collection of equally bland high-end thrift store finds), her dark brown hair was pulled back in her typical stern bun.

Though sometimes she indulged in a "messy" bun, she had never once, not even when she worked in the mail room, worn her long hair loose.

Since coming to work for Liam, she always wore glasses. Today, the pair she had chosen were particularly heavily framed. In addition, Molly had allowed herself only a hint of lip gloss and eye makeup. Just enough to be professional in her upscale office, not enough to draw attention.

And despite all that, there it was, that look in his eye as if he *saw* her, completely. Of course, by now she knew that was one of the many gifts Liam brought to this business.

He made people feel seen and important. And there was not a single thing put-on about it. His skyrocket of success was, at least in part, because of his very genuine interest in his fellow man.

And for Molly, there was nothing like authenticity to up her crush factor. Though his scent didn't help. His aroma was distinctly his. In the very center of all the action and mayhem and energy that made up New York City, Liam smelled of forests, hidden valleys and waterfalls.

She resisted an urge to tuck an escaped strand of dark hair behind her ear and to run a tongue over her lips. Both gestures would probably be a dead giveaway.

Executive assistant, falling hard and fast. Well, she told herself, sternly and firmly, in the he-makes-women-giddy department, she could get in line with the rest of the world!

"Sunday," Liam said, after a moment of studying her. "You look distressed. I hate it when you look distressed."

She'd been working for FIX for eighteen months, and for Liam directly for the last six. She'd come to his attention after she had made a suggestion in the mail room that had upped the efficiency of that department considerably.

At first, she'd been an assistant to his assistant, but Maxine had decided she wanted to devote herself to her new grandbabies, twins with some minor health issues. So, somehow, three months ago Molly had found herself stepping into her predecessor's shoes.

In truth, she had never had a job she loved so much, or that she felt so devoted to. She'd come from a childhood world of absolute chaos, and so bringing order to a complicated life felt as if it was the very thing she had been born to do.

She had referred to herself, early on in her new position, as his Girl Friday, and he had considered it with a tilt of his head.

"I don't like that term," he'd said, after a moment.

"Why? It comes from the name of Robinson Crusoe's assistant on the deserted island. And then, that theme was played on in a 1940s movie called *His Girl Friday*."

"Is there anything you don't know?" he'd asked.

"Of course there are things I don't know!"

"Huh. Who wrote Robinson Crusoe?"

"Daniel Defoe."

"What day did the Titanic sink?"

This was a little game they played often, both of them enjoying it equally.

"April 15, 1912. The vessel sank four days into her maiden voyage."

"See?" he said, with a satisfied sigh. "How do you do that? Oh, wait! You told me. You read. And you know things."

That didn't tell half the story, of course. The full story was a childhood of coming second to her brother, Donnie, in an environment of chronic poverty, chaos and addiction.

And into all that, the discovery of a library and a kindhearted librarian, Mrs. Deverille. A discovery of the escapes offered the very second one opened a page. Any page. Of any book. And in that small library Molly had learned to read anything she could get her hands on.

"The next time I play trivia, I want you as a partner."

But, of course, as the recent keeper of his schedule, Molly knew Liam's life did not exactly have room for playing trivia and that there was no being his partner—in any sense of the word—anywhere in her future. Or his. Even early on, she'd known not to complicate the best job she had ever had.

"It really only refers to an indispensable assistant, male or female," Molly had told him. "There's nothing derogatory about it."

"No, I disagree," he'd said. "The whole Friday thing. There's something vaguely master to servant about it that I don't like. Are you indispensable? Yes."

The crush had probably started that second of being told she was indispensable, being *seen* as valuable and with something to offer.

No, that was a lie. The crush had probably started the moment she had laid eyes on him, even back in her mail room days. All the women who worked here had crushes on him. It was perfectly harmless.

Until it wasn't.

CHAPTER TWO

THAT'S WHAT MOLLY had kept in mind when Liam had regarded her so solemnly as he weighed in on the nickname Girl Friday.

"My servant?" he had said, then added firmly, "No."

"How about Sunday, then?" she'd kidded him, then as now, eager to hide how he was making her feel behind many layers, humor being one of them.

"Sunday." He'd considered it. "You do work Sundays. And it's in keeping with your ability to pull off absolute miracles. Okay, Sunday it is."

She gave him a little mock salute.

He considered for a moment. "But only if you call me Saturday."

They'd laughed then. That had been the first time in their working relationship they had laughed together, and really, if she looked for the little sparks of her ridiculous crush on him being fanned more dangerously to life, that exchange would definitely rate.

He did call her Sunday. But she only called him Saturday on the rarest of occasions, because it seemed way too familiar. Still, he absolutely would not stand for her calling him *Mr. Westerhouse* or *sir.*

Molly also found the familiarity of calling him Liam uncomfortable, so she settled on *boss*, or sometimes *chief.*

"So, Sunday," he said, "why the look of distress? Not much rattles you."

"Well, we find you without a date for Innovators on the Move. Which begins in—" she glanced at the wall clock "—one hour and fifty-three minutes."

"Ah." He seemed singularly unperturbed. "Who was it supposed to be?"

"Eva La Lydia."

Eva La Lydia was arguably one of the most beautiful women in the world. Her boss, endearingly, wrinkled his nose and grimaced.

"The name alone," he said, with a rueful shake of his head. "Awful. Whose idea was that?"

"The name? Or the arrangement for her to accompany you to the event?"

"The name, even though the origins of the name are probably obscure—"

"Not really. Her real name is Evelyn Lyndall. After being discovered playing Fantine in her high school production of *Les Misérables*, she thought a French take on her name would make her a standout as she pursued her acting career."

He didn't ask how she knew, but of course she was going to do a bit of basic research on anyone he was being paired with.

He pointed to his chest and then her. "See?" he said. "You and me and trivia. We could take on the world, Sunday. Okay. Question two: whose idea was it to set me up with *her* for the evening?"

She was glad she could not take credit for that one.

"Francis Whittaker, from publicity. Miss La Lydia is the star of *Yellow Rock*. Being seen with her would bring plenty of coverage to both the young innovators and to FIX."

"Ah, well," he said, "I'm sure FIX will limp along without the exposure. Sorry about the young innovators having to settle for just me, though."

He grinned at her, and he looked so impossibly charming she had to steel herself against the flutter of her heart.

"I should warn you," she said firmly, determined to keep it all business, "Miss La Lydia has said she's going to complain to you personally. About me."

"She doesn't have my phone number, does she?" Liam asked, alarmed.

"Not on my watch," Molly said, emphatically.

"Good job, Sunday. What's her complaint?"

"She didn't like my attitude."

"Your attitude?"

Molly consulted her notes. "Rude and snippy, to be exact. She wouldn't sign the NDA, and so I told her the evening was off. She has a record of kiss and tell."

She kept her eyes firmly on her notes. For a few

seconds. Then, despite her legendary discipline, she couldn't resist sneaking a peek at him.

And the part of him responsible for kisses.

Would he have kissed Eva? She cast about in herself for questionable motives. Was she guarding him, even subconsciously, from other women's kisses? Was that why she'd called off the evening?

Of course not! It was all about the NDA.

"I take full responsibility," Molly said, "for the evening not turning out. I really should have made sure the NDA was in order, sooner."

"Ha. It sounds as if we dodged a bullet, really."

We.

Molly was aware of this horrible ability she had developed to make something out of nothing.

"How could I spend a whole evening with someone willing to think one bad thought about my Woman Sunday?"

There was that feeling. That wonderful feeling of someone having your back. You could not risk that on something as ridiculous—and hopefully fleeting—as a crush.

"Thanks, boss," Molly said. "Of course, Miss La Lydia would have been great publicity for FIX, as Francis knew when she set it up. She's the It girl, right now."

Again, she saw a slight flattening around Liam's mouth, as if he had known all along that the image the star projected was not at all who she was.

Well, he would know. He had been seen with

some of the most beautiful and famous women in the world. None seemed to impress him.

If there was one thing she knew for certain about Liam's personal life, it was that he didn't really have one. His relationship was with his business.

And he was absolutely committed to being single.

Still, that required doing this delicate dance with the media. Publicity was good for the business. They played on Liam's star quality all the time. The fact that he was twenty-eight and single worked in their favor, because women *adored* him.

He'd twice been featured in a very well-known publication as their choice for Bachelor of the Year.

But it was also a balancing act to keep his life private, and to allow him to give most of his focus to what he did best, which was running an incredible business.

Liam, in defiance of his family's traditions and old money, had pursued his own interests and become a mechanical engineer. While he was in university his parents had been killed in a plane crash. He'd inherited an absolute fortune and could have easily given up his education and gone on to live the lifestyle of the rich and famous, acting as honorary CEO for the family business, Westerhouse Group.

Instead, he had completed his education, graduated with a master's degree, and without touching his inheritance, he had founded FIX (Find Innovative eXcellence). It had started small, but he'd discovered a missing component in an aerospace project, and developed a solution that had brought him incredible notice and propelled him toward success.

Since then, absolute brilliance, discipline and energy had created a meteoric rise of the company. Liam brought his incredible abilities, vigour and enthusiasm to finding solutions and creating products in a wide-ranging number of industries, including manufacturing, aerospace, automotive, construction, energy and biomedical.

"So, I can try and find a last-minute for you," Molly volunteered, "or you can go solo. I'm afraid ducking out isn't an option as the company is one of the sponsors and you're one of the presenters."

"Up-and-Comer of the Year." He patted his suit pocket. "I have my speech right here. As per your notes: award goes to Jordan Houston, inventor of Fresh, a portable device that can convert fouled water to fresh and has unbelievable potential in natural disaster areas."

"You make my job so easy," she said.

"No, you make my job easy. I know, by the way, your job is not easy. It's hard. And somehow you make it seem like every day, no matter what I throw at you, is an absolute delight."

Dangerous to bask in his approval! She moved on rapidly.

"So, boss, solo or should I find someone?"

"I'm not really familiar with many of the people in that organization," he said. "I have an unfortunate picture of sitting at a big banquet table by myself, twiddling my thumbs."

She was pretty sure he'd be surrounded by admirers in seconds, though no doubt that could be as difficult as sitting alone.

"It'll remind me of my unhappy younger self," he said. "The little outcast who sat by himself through meals for all my private school years. Though sometimes I just bypassed the mess hall and ate in the kitchen with the cook. She loved me after I fixed the commercial dishwasher that had given her grief for years."

Every now and then, *this*. This precious glimpse of what had made Liam Westerhouse so different from so many others who had been born into the kind of wealth he had been born into.

He was a good role model for someone like her. *You could mine your past for strength and resilience.*

She thought of the latest phone call from her mother and shuddered. Well, maybe not *her* past.

They needed more money for Donnie's latest legal battle. It was not his first one, but it was by far the most serious.

Molly thought about her younger brother. He had been the hope of a family abandoned by their father. In the mess of desperation and bitterness dear old Dad had left in his wake, Donnie had been the rising star, the bright shining one she and her mother had pinned their hopes on.

Her brother was good-looking, had ample easygoing Southern charm and was extraordinarily athletic. The colleges started scouting him when he was still a junior in high school. He was National

Football League material and everybody knew he was going to be a star—he was going to put their little backwater bayou on the map.

He was their ticket out. Molly learned only his needs mattered. She was there to serve the king of their household.

And then, he was injured, at a practice. A broken shoulder. A family without medical insurance. Donnie given opiates to control the pain.

Instead of their ticket out, he had completed the Littleton family's spiral downward.

And yet, her mother could not let go of her vision of Donnie. She continued to pour her adoration—and the family's very limited resources—on Donnie. She continued to treat Molly as if her only job on earth was to shore up her brother.

Escape to New York had given Molly the physical distance she so desperately needed, but the mental bonds were harder to break.

Donnie had been caught in the wrong place at the wrong time, according to her mother's latest call, her words increasingly slurred as the call progressed.

He had nothing to do with the armed robbery of Baskin's liquor store. Donnie had only been walking by. He was an innocent victim in the whole thing.

He's going to go to jail, her mother had wailed, *if we can't pay a good lawyer. You should see what you get for free. He'll be in jail for the rest of his life if we have to use the public defender. Do you know what happens to good-looking boys like him in jail?*

Molly wondered what Liam would think if he

knew about *that*. What anyone here at FIX would think if they knew the truth about the prim, proper and entirely professional Miss Littleton's ongoing dramas with a family plunged into poverty, desperation and hopelessness that had started when the last auto plant had pulled out of Shreveport, and decades later, showed no signs of ending.

Her mother seemed only to resent the fact Molly had managed to escape it all, as if her abandonment was identical to their father's and as if Molly had left her mother and Donnie to be devoured in an alligator-infested swamp. Though that resentment didn't keep either her brother or her mother from treating her like the Bank of Molly.

And her guilt about leaving them all behind—about loving her new life so darned much—kept her writing the checks.

No wonder she had developed an unrealistic crush on her boss. If ever there had been a girl who needed a fairy tale, it was Molly!

Still, she'd grown up with enough hard knocks that she'd known you could open the pages of a story and escape there, but you had to tread that fine line of not investing in dreams too deeply. Hope, after all, was the most dangerous thing of all.

"Don't you have someone you can call?" she asked Liam, and inserted a light note into her voice as she added, marveling at the fact she was in a position to tease him, "'World's Most Eligible Bachelor'?"

CHAPTER THREE

MOLLY LOVED IT when Liam wrinkled his nose, which he did now, at being reminded he was considered one of the world's most eligible bachelors. "I'm not currently seeing anyone."

Which, of course, as keeper of his social calendar, Molly knew.

In the eighteen months she had worked for the company, and the three since she'd had total reign over his personal schedule, Liam had never been seeing anyone. He seemed more than content to let his staff figure out companions for him when he needed an escort for an event.

These were always, as far as Molly could tell, one-offs. He never asked her to find him a phone number, never requested any follow-up information.

"Married to my job," he'd said to her once, cheerfully. "The best partner ever."

She could see this was true. Liam Westerhouse was married to his job. He worked relentlessly. In his world there were no weekends. He was usually at his office in the morning before she got there, and he was often back there at night as she was getting ready to leave.

Molly had chided him once, that he was working too hard.

"Working?" he'd said with genuine surprise. "I'm not working, Sunday. I'm playing."

His social calendar was jam-packed, but only with events that benefited or forwarded the cause of FIX or one of the many organizations and charities that FIX supported.

"I'll try and find someone," she said. "So you don't have to sit alone. It's very short notice, though, so no guarantees."

"Maybe I'll just bow out."

She gnawed her lip. "I don't think they could find another presenter on such short notice. I researched Jordan and she really hopes to work for FIX one day. I think she'd be devastated if you didn't show up."

"Probably any representative from the company would do."

"It's pretty short notice, chief."

Liam contemplated that, and then brightened.

"Sunday," he said. "You'd be perfect for the job."

"What job?" she stammered.

"You could do it!" he said. He tried to pass her his notes for his speech. "You've already done the homework. You know about the award winner. You'd be a perfect representative of FIX."

"No," she said vehemently, shifting her chair away from the papers he held out to her.

"Oh—" he gave himself a smack on the forehead "—how thoughtless of me to think you'd be any more comfortable sitting alone than I would be."

"That's not it," she said.

"What is it, then?"

"Really? I'm a nobody. From Liam Westerhouse and Eva La Lydia, to me?"

He looked stunned by that. He cocked his head and narrowed his eyes. It felt as if he was seeing her differently than how he normally did.

"A nobody?" he said, something dangerous in his tone.

"I mean not a celebrity. Not a person of note."

"You are not a nobody," he said, that same dangerous note in his voice.

She thought of her mother and brother. If only he knew! She realized she felt like an imposter. Even though she had spent countless hours taming that telltale touch of the South from her voice, poring over magazines to figure out how to look "right" for an upscale office, investing money in pedicures and manicures—things scorned in her childhood neighborhood—she still had this awful feeling someday she was going to be caught.

"Never mind," he said, and he seemed to be in rare ill humor. "Just cancel it. I'll make it up to the kid getting the award. She could come for a tour of the company. I'll take her for lunch or something."

She thought of Liam's jam-packed schedule.

Where was she going to fit that in? She could feel a little headache gathering between her eyes, right over the bridge of her nose.

"How about if I go with you?" she said, impulsively.

She reminded herself she was not impulsive. There was always a price to be paid for being impulsive.

"Like pretend to be my date?" he asked, astonished.

"No, no, nothing like that!" She was blushing wildly.

"Oh," he said, snapping his fingers. "Like my plus-one."

"That sounds like an unfortunate dress size," she said.

He laughed.

As soon as Liam laughed, Molly was aware her intent in offering her services for the evening had not been completely pure. It wasn't about finding a lunch slot in a tight schedule. And it wasn't just about being helpful in a new way, either.

No, she wanted to spend more time with him.

She was being greedy for his company, pure and simple.

And she, of all people, should know about the dangers involved in wanting *more.*

"*Plus-one* is just a phrase people use," Liam said to her. "It just means a kind of no-strings-attached companion for an event."

"Oh," she said. His having to explain it to her

just reminded her more how she had never really been in the mainstream, not like the sophisticated people he generally hung out with.

Liam cocked his head, considering. "Sunday, it's an absolutely brilliant suggestion, no matter what we call it. You don't have to give a speech; I don't have to eat alone."

She felt compelled to clarify. "I'll just be your assistant, as always."

"Exactly! But people won't know that. It'll look like you're my date—"

"Plus-one," she inserted, and earned his grin.

"And as a bonus, with none of the complications that come from a real date."

"Complications?" she said, uncertainly.

"You know. To kiss or not to kiss."

The very question that she had wondered about for his date with Eva! It was an unfair invitation to look at his lips, again. The downward swooping of her stomach told her that far from being brilliant, this was possibly the dumbest idea she'd ever had.

"You know," she said, weakly, "maybe I didn't think it through."

"How very unlike you," he said, that lovely mouth quirking upward, again, in that hint of a smile a Girl Sunday—or a plus-one—could live for.

"Agreed," she said, and his smile turned to a laugh at her sullenness.

"I'm sorry," Liam said. "Did you just realize you had other plans?"

It just went to show, Molly thought, that while

she knew practically everything there was to know about him, Liam knew next to nothing about her. Wasn't it evident that she did not have other plans? Wasn't it evident that work—and a good book on her bedside table—were her life?

The consequences of her wanting more were just beginning to sink in. The truth was the less he knew about her the better and this impulsive invitation was opening territory she did not want opened.

Besides, it would be more than evident to anyone who saw them together she was outmatched. That no matter how much time she spent on her accent, no matter how carefully she selected clothes from the thrift store, no matter how much money she spent on manicures and pedicures, she could not belong in the world he moved in so easily—a world of money, sophistication, power.

"It's not that I have another plan," she said, though how she wished she had a handsome man and tickets to a Broadway show to fall back on. "It's just I'm not dressed for an event like that, and I don't live close enough to go change."

As if she had a dress that would work for a function like that, even if she did live close enough to go change.

"Where do you live?" he asked, puzzled.

See? This was the door she had opened. One ill thought-out statement and she had invited this peek into her personal life that had not happened in the time since she'd become his assistant.

"I have a little place in Marine Park."

"Marine Park?"

"Brooklyn."

"Isn't that a long commute?"

"It's not bad. Forty-five minutes. I like the subway."

"What?"

This was the problem with sashaying over the line into the personal. Now she had to avoid telling him that every single thing about New York was a miracle to her, from having a tiny, peaceful basement suite, to riding the subway with other people who were on their way to ordinary jobs that they totally took for granted.

He considered that, and then asked, carefully, "Do you need a raise?"

Sometimes, despite how humble he usually was, despite his being the boy who had eaten in his school kitchen with the cook, being raised with a lot of money showed. He couldn't believe anyone in the world who had a choice wouldn't live in Manhattan. He was obviously incredulous—even though he was trying to hide it—that anyone enjoyed the subway.

Had he ever even been on the subway?

She resisted the temptation to ask. "No, I do not need a raise!"

"Are you sure? Because you have been putting in a lot of hours on the weekends, too."

"I'm sure." The truth was she would probably pay him to work at his company if she had to and she was already stunned by the amount of money she was making. FIX was inordinately good to all its employees. In fact, she could have a small place in Manhattan if she wasn't bankrolling her current family disaster.

There was that deliciously sexy upward quirk of his mouth again.

"There you go, Sunday, the one-in-a-million person who would say they don't need a raise."

He looked so genuinely appreciative of her.

Don't preen, she ordered herself. If there was one thing her childhood had taught her, it was to not get distracted from dealing with the crisis at hand.

"Anyway, I don't have anything to wear, and I don't want to embarrass you, so—"

"Embarrass me? Oh, Sunday. You could be wearing a flour sack dress and everything you are would still shine through."

She winced at that, though not the shining-through part. The flour sack part. Because Liam Westerhouse didn't have any real clue what a flour sack dress was. She, on the other hand, had a worn picture tucked in her top bureau drawer of ancestors wearing those dresses, staring into a camera, defeated, and resentful of their horrible circumstances being captured on film.

He eyed her thoughtfully for a moment, and then waved a hand at her. "Clothes are easy. If having something to wear is your only worry, let's go get you something."

Of course not being dressed appropriately was not her only worry. *This* was her worry: stepping into more uncharted territory with her boss. Once the line between personal and professional blurred, was there any putting it back?

It felt as if, if she now invested in this plan that she had very stupidly suggested—here were the consequences of impulsivity—she could wreck the perfect life she had maneuvered her way into, disturb the precious balance she had so carefully created and controlled.

And wasn't that the very legacy she was trying to outrun?

Littletons had a special gift for snatching defeat from the jaws of victory, for turning blessings into curses.

She knew she had to back away from this.

Say no, Molly told herself. Go home to her tiny, cozy apartment, her book and a fussy African violet she had named Winspear. Well, probably not the book, tonight. Liam had a trip to Québec City coming up next week and she had not taken care of the final details.

She knew something about Liam that hardly anyone knew. He *loved* chocolate. And so somehow this had become one of her things: Before he left on a trip, she researched all the local chocolatiers and made sure a selection of the very best the region had to offer was available in his hotel room. She always did it on her own time, as it didn't really fall under the purview of her duties. She paid for it herself. It made it feel like her gift to him, a way of expressing some of her pent-up feelings without saying a word.

He didn't seem to have caught on that she was behind the chocolate. She had begun waiting with anticipation for his return, because inevitably, he would say, "Sunday, you've got to try this."

Thinking of the interesting evening ahead of her, Molly glanced at her watch and made another excuse.

So much easier, somehow, to safely indulge her secret crush from a distance. "I'm pretty sure most of the shops are on the brink of closing."

His phone was out of his pocket in a flash. "I have a friend."

Oh. *Now*, he had a friend. But five minutes ago, when he'd needed someone to go with him to the awards dinner, *nada*.

"I'll ask them to stay open for an extra hour. What do you say?"

Liam was really offering her a kind of Cinderella experience. And though she was a long way, physically, from her roots, the girl of rags and ashes lived on inside her.

A girl who had longed, powerfully, for fairy tales.

Really, she was living a fairy tale. Dream job. New York City. Distance from her crazy family. Little apartment. Even her plant was thriving. It was all so blissfully domestic. Normal. Except for that one part.

Secretly in love with her boss.

She had to kill this tiny, persistent longing for more. That was one lesson she needed to carry from her hardscrabble childhood. Don't wish for too much. Don't dance with boldness. Don't take chances.

There was safety in invisibility.

Say no, Molly ordered herself.

Instead, of its own volition, her shoulder lifted as if it was the most casual of decisions, as if she wasn't playing fast and loose with the very thing that had given her happiness—her career.

She heard herself say, as if she was one of those breezy, fun-loving girls capable of being impulsive, "Sure. Why not?"

Fifth Avenue was buzzing as Molly and Liam made their way down a crowded sidewalk. It was early spring and New York was shaking off the gray winter doldrums.

Coming from a small town, she loved this delicious combination of energy and anonymity.

Not that it was so anonymous with Liam at her side. In a city where no one looked at each other, it seemed everyone looked at him.

Some people, of course, would recognize him.

But it was more his sheer presence that attracted so many glances, and a few boldly inviting gazes.

Liam didn't appear to notice, taking her elbow on occasion to guide her through the worst crush of the crowds.

And then he was holding open the door of a boutique aptly named Second Chances. As the door closed behind them, Molly felt the hush, in sharp contrast to the bustle outside.

She had walked by this business many times and even allowed herself to wonder about going in, but she never had. It was not just a boutique but a complete makeover service.

She slid Liam a look. Did he think she needed that? A complete makeover?

Of course he did! No one wanted a plus-one, even a fake plus-one, who wasn't quite up to standard.

The entry lobby was beautiful—a subtle pay station at its center, with a lighted wall of extraordinary before-and-after portraits behind it. The transformations people experienced here were nothing short of stunning.

The motto was etched on the desk in silver relief.

Don't change who you are, ever. But embrace every single thing you were meant to be.

She wasn't sure that bold statement included young women from the wrong side of the tracks in Louisiana.

For a moment, she considered bolting out the door. She could feel the ground shifting under her feet. She could feel something coming; she could smell it the way an animal can smell a storm coming on the wind. And it was the thing she hated the most.

Change.

Almost as if he sensed her discomfort, Liam ever so lightly touched her arm. The perfect “plus-one” touch. Without a word that touch said, *Hey, we’re in this together. I got you.*

The change wasn’t coming, she realized. It wasn’t a flash of lightning off in the distance. With that light touch, it was *here*. The storm was breaking.

CHAPTER FOUR

LIAM SENSED SOME CHANGE in Molly almost the second they walked through the door of Second Chances. He slid her a glance, trying to figure out what the shift was.

She looked, really, as she always did. She was wearing one of those box-like suits she preferred, and sensible shoes. Her dark hair was scraped back into a stern no-nonsense bun, which for some reason accentuated how glossy it was, and how it was completely untouched by artificial color. The color of her hair reminded him, suddenly, of melted dark chocolate.

Those glasses made her look endearingly earnest and owlish. But just as for some reason her hairstyle made him more aware of how glossy those strands were, the glasses that he suspected were intended to make her seem serious always made him aware of how stunningly blue her eyes were.

There hadn't been girls at his private school, but Liam had come to see Molly's type later in university. The ones who hugged huge piles of books against their chests, avoided eye contact and seemed most at home in the library.

He certainly had not given a thought at the time to what valuable employees those studious, seemingly intent-on-being-invisible young women would become.

From those first days, when Molly had come into his office under the wing of Maxine, he'd seen what her gift was.

Complete competence.

Molly simply radiated reliability. In a very short time he'd come to find her indispensable, with her razor-sharp intelligence and her amazing organizational skills.

He'd never seen her caught out, never seen a challenge upset her or defeat her.

She was imminently trustworthy. Was that why he'd blurted that out about eating in the kitchen with the cook? He was not sure he'd ever shared that with anyone before.

But now he was aware that something had happened as soon as they walked in the door of this boutique. At a glance, it wasn't that noticeable. He saw her studying the pictures behind the desk and realized, for the first time, that this wasn't just a boutique. It was some kind of makeover place.

Was that the cause of the fine tension around her mouth and in her eyes? Was that why her shoulders were ever so faintly hunched forward, as though she wanted to disappear? He noticed her arm was stiffly at her side, but that she was rubbing her index finger against her thumb together nervously.

"Hey, I didn't know about that," he assured her with a nod toward the pictures. "I just thought it was a place to pick up a dress."

Despite his clumsy attempt to make her realize he approved of her just the way she was, the smile she gave him seemed strained.

He realized Molly Littleton, his Woman Sunday, his executive assistant extraordinaire, was a duck out of water.

A man came out of an alcove off the main reception area.

"Mr. Westerhouse," he said, extending his hand, "a pleasure. I'm Christopher."

"I appreciate you staying open. We've had a sudden shift in plans and my assistant wasn't sure her current outfit would work. This is Molly Littleton. I've pressed her into extra duties tonight. She's unexpectedly attending an awards dinner with me, with a cocktail event to follow, so she needs to choose a dress."

"We'll have something perfect," Christopher assured them smoothly.

Molly did not look reassured. "I wouldn't even know what I'm looking for." Her voice seemed high and uncertain.

Liam stared at her. His Molly? Who could handle anything? His Sunday, who had just put some full-of-herself starlet firmly in her place, felled by a dress?

"Ask her anything," Liam suggested, trying to find familiar ground to put her at ease. "She's my superpower. A walking encyclopedia."

Christopher played along, guiding Molly toward the boutique area. "When was America discovered?"

"Too easy," Liam said, following close behind them as if he might have to prevent a full bolt toward the door.

"*Discovered* has become a slightly contentious term," Molly said, and she did sound relieved and grateful to be on more familiar footing, "but Christopher—oh, possibly your namesake—Columbus landed in the Americas on the island now known as the Bahamas in 1492. He was thought to be the first European but actually his arrival was predated by several centuries by the Viking explorer, Leif Erikson."

Liam wagged his eyebrows at Christopher. "See?"

Christopher tilted his head at Molly. "I could swear I hear the faintest trace of the South in your accent," he said.

Any confidence being back on familiar footing had given Molly evaporated. She had a sudden deer-in-the-headlights look.

Again, Liam was aware how different she was outside of the office environment. She was so sure of herself in that realm, radiating confidence and certainty and utter competence.

He had never detected any kind of accent in his

assistant. He thought she would confirm or deny Christopher's observation but instead she was silent. It occurred to him part of the reason Molly was so good at her job was that she seemed most comfortable staying in the background.

It also occurred to him how very little he knew about her personally. Though he'd found out two new things about her today—three if you counted Christopher's observation about her accent.

Molly didn't like the spotlight. Really, he should have known that from the understated way that she dressed at the office.

But, even more surprisingly, he'd discovered she wasn't motivated by money. She'd vehemently turned down his offer to compensate her more.

These observations were hitting him like a breath of fresh air. In other words, Molly was the absolute antithesis of every other woman who had been his plus-one in the past few years.

And certainly the antithesis of Charlotte Weeby, a woman he had narrowly escaped marrying.

Charlie. What some people would call a gold digger. He felt that familiar rush of anger, not so much at her for betraying him, but at himself for being so naive, so blind to who she really was, so desperate for love…

He snapped himself out of that train of thought.

All the more reason that Molly was absolutely perfect to be his plus-one. He wondered, a bit guiltily, if he'd been so enamored with how she'd performed her job that he had really failed to see her more deeply.

Well, here was his chance to make it up to her. What woman didn't love an all-expenses-paid shopping trip?

Apparently Molly. She looked terrified by the array of choices displayed on the racks of clothing in the boutique they had entered. She moved to a rack, hesitantly, and turned over a tag.

Her look of terror deepened.

"Of course I'm paying," he said, stunned that she would reach any other conclusion. Again, the opposite of anyone else he'd gone out with.

A look flashed across her face: something proud and obstinate.

"You don't need to buy me a dress, chief."

"It's a business excursion," he said. "Completely unexpected."

The stubborn look deepened on her face. "Working in the office is business, too, and I don't expect you to provide me with a wardrobe."

The truth was he'd provide her with a thousand wardrobes if it guaranteed her happiness as his employee.

"When I asked you to go to our office in Los Angeles last month," he said reasonably, "did you buy your own ticket?"

She looked suddenly worried, as if maybe she *should* have bought her own ticket.

It was everything he could do not to hit himself in the forehead with his fist.

She turned away from him and squinted at the dress selections. She did that little thing where she gnawed on her lip while she thought about it.

When had he come to love that *thing* so much?

"Okay," she said. "Once. And then I'll have something to wear. You know. In case."

She was blushing.

"In case?"

"You know, in case it ever came up again. That you needed me to play your plus-one."

"Sunday, you're giving me a headache. Could you just pick a dress?"

"Speaking of brand-new worlds," she said, nervously. "Where do you begin?"

Now that it had been pointed out, he could hear the faintest of accents, and he found it unsettling that it hinted at parts of his seemingly straightforward assistant that he knew nothing about.

And whatever that was, in that faint accent, it suddenly seemed mysterious, and dangerously sensual.

"I think you'll find your size in this section," Christopher said.

Liam watched, bemused, at his unflappable assistant being so flustered over this. A dress. She plowed her hands into the rack, flipped through a few dresses, then yanked one out.

She held it up in front of her. "I'll try this one."

Liam stared at the dress, aghast. It had large patterned purple flowers all over it and a lace collar. It reminded him of something the mother had worn on a reality television show he had watched once—only once—who had had far too many children. He slid Christopher a look.

His ever so competent assistant was now staring at her choice, looking as if she knew what a terrible mistake the dress was and did not know how to back down. Oh, geez. Was her lip trembling?

"You'll have to try on more than one," Christopher said smoothly.

She turned back to the rack like a prisoner being forced to choose her own punishment and began reluctantly, and a bit frantically, sorting through more dresses.

"Why don't we each choose one for you?" Christopher suggested, easily. "You, me and your boss? And you can try them all on, and see which one you like best."

Each choose one? Liam was going to choose a dress for Molly? He hoped she would say no, she was quite capable of choosing her own dress. But he did not get off the hook that easily. She actually looked relieved by Christopher's suggestion!

The moment seemed surreal, as Liam stood at her shoulder, thumbing through the choices.

Surely he had stood this close to her before? Why hadn't he ever noticed her scent?

Spicy. Mysterious. Sensual.

Just like some place in the Deep South that he hadn't known about.

Liam felt as if the weight of the world was on his shoulders as he carefully skimmed through the dress selection. The choice suddenly seemed fraught with complications.

He did not want her to think there was anything wrong with the way she was.

He did not want to choose something inappropriately sexy.

Or horribly dull, either.

"This one," he said decisively, finally settling on what felt like a very safe choice. Some memory of his mother getting ready to go out tickled. *You can never go wrong with the basic little black dress.*

He held up a very plain dress for Molly's inspection. The look on her face was wounded, as if he had chosen a nun's habit.

She snatched it from his hand, and added it to the hanger she already held aloft, far away from her, as if the clothing items were fish that smelled bad.

Christopher, thankfully, had the most experience at this. He carefully picked a dress in bronze, and then he relieved Molly of the other two and led her to the fitting area. Molly trailed him.

Liam wasn't sure what he was supposed to do, which for a decisive man was not a comfortable situation to be in.

She shot him a look over her shoulder and the faint pleading in it—*how on earth do we find ourselves here*—made him ever so reluctantly follow her.

What was he supposed to do? Surely not weigh in on her choices? Somehow the plus-one thing, which had at first glance seemed like such a perfect solution, had become unexpectedly complicated.

Liam sighed and sat down in a deep chair that Christopher motioned him toward.

But wasn't that the nature of charades, even ones that were extremely well-intentioned?

Unexpected complexities arose. It was the way of them.

CHAPTER FIVE

"YOU'RE NOT GOING to the gallows," Christopher admonished her, in an undertone, as he tucked her into a spacious change cubicle with the dresses. "Most women would *love* this."

As the door clicked closed behind him, Molly contemplated how she would absolutely love to be *most women* right now. But she simply wasn't. She never had been. She'd always been an outsider in *that* world of matching your fingernail polish to your lipstick, of giggling over boys, of knowing what was trendy and of being comfortable and familiar with the phrases of the day.

Like *plus-one* for instance.

She thought she had found a place at FIX where her inherent unusualness was a good fit. Maybe even her strength. Now, her world felt horribly off-kilter. In jeopardy, even.

She put her back against that door and took a deep breath.

She was panicking. For goodness' sake, it was a dress, not trying to find a lifeboat aboard the *Titanic*. On April 15, 1912.

Still, her boss, yes, the very one she had a secret crush on, was right outside, settling onto one of those sofas. She was grateful for a real door. Not a flimsy curtain.

Was that what was causing the sensation of panic? That she was going to be standing in her underwear just a few feet from him, separated only by an insubstantial door?

Or was the panic because Christopher had noticed her accent. So what? It wasn't as if he'd sent out an announcement card: *trailer trash.*

No, maybe it was because she'd slipped up and suggested the plus-one thing might happen again.

Had she sounded happy?

Of course she hadn't sounded happy! So far, this new experience with her boss felt like her worst nightmare. To add to the sense of being overwhelmed, which she had felt from the moment she walked in the doors of Second Chances, shopping for dresses with her boss—him insisting he would pay—all this just felt way too weird and way too intimate.

And this change-up in her routine was too catastrophically sudden, especially for someone who liked planning as much as she did. It was a plunge from her regular life into *this*—modelling dresses for a fake date with her boss—in the blink of an eye. It was like falling through ice into a lake when you thought you were on solid, dry land.

Molly glanced at her watch and gulped. They were now one hour and thirteen minutes from the awards dinner. One hour and three minutes if they arrived at least ten minutes early, which, of course, they should.

There was no time for self-doubt. No time for rumination. She had to approach this as a soldier on a mission, a soldier with orders from her commanding officer.

Taking one final deep breath, Molly discarded her clothes. She caught a glimpse of herself in the mirror. Her underwear was pristinely clean, of course, but she was aware it was both worn and extremely utilitarian. She was pretty sure she'd had this bra since high school.

She blew her limited clothing budget on outer trimmings, and even pre-used designer items were expensive, particularly when you were trying to keep your brother out of jail.

No one—except Winspear—was ever exposed to her undies, anyway.

When had she started thinking of Winspear, her African violet, as if it was a roommate?

That, along with the picture she cut in her worn undies—her extraordinarily well-put-together boss sitting mere feet away, his underwear no doubt as extraordinary as he himself was—left Molly with a clear evaluation of herself.

Pathetic.

And now, she had allowed a totally inappropriate thought about Liam's underwear, and even as she mentally forbade herself to go down that road, a little voice inside her insisted on asking—

But what do you think? Boxers or briefs?

She pulled on the first dress with just a little more force than might have been absolutely necessary. It was her choice, the purple one. As she yanked it over her head, her hair pulled partly out of its bun.

She glared at her image in the mirror. The dress was like a bride's choice for a bridesmaid she didn't particularly like.

The shoes were so wrong. She kicked them off.

Standing there barefoot, with her falling-down hair, and the dress settling around her like a *flour* sack, she looked every inch the girl from the trailer park trying with a pathetic desperation to fit in where everyone knew she didn't belong.

"This one won't work," she called. Was she going to cry?

"The purple one?" Christopher asked, knowingly. "With the collar?"

"Yes."

"Try on the bronze."

She didn't want to try on another dress! She wanted to go home and water Winspear and open her file on Liam's upcoming trip. There were things to do, comforting things, like double-checking with the pilot and making sure the hotel had upgraded the suite.

Still, they were on a time frame, so screwing up what little courage remained, Molly did as she was told. The dress slid on over her head like a whisper and fell down around her, to her feet. She wrestled with the long zipper for a bit, and with every inch it went up, Molly became aware she had never worn anything that *felt* like this dress. As if it was hugging her.

She turned and stared at herself in the mirror, stunned. Her sense of being pathetic vanished.

Was she really that superficial? The entire way she felt about herself could be fixed with a dress?

Well, a gorgeous dress, but nonetheless… The dress shimmered, its V-neck delicately sensual, rather than overtly sexual. It was formfitting to the waist, where it snugged in hard, before it flared out in a cloudy dream.

Her hair suddenly didn't look messy. It looked—did she dare say it—slightly chic. Even the bare feet didn't matter.

She reminded herself that this was what Second Chances did, what Christopher did every single day.

This business, and its consultants, turned ordinary people into the best version of themselves, the version they might not have even known was there.

She felt transformed, indeed a Cinderella story—barefoot trailer park girl to princess in the wave of a wand. But what no one ever said was how discombobulating a Cinderella experience was. How much it made you aware of *pretense*, the underwear just underneath it probably being a more true reflection of who she was.

Still, there was no denying it felt a bit like the

dress in the dance scene of *Beauty and the Beast*. Transformational.

"Well?" Christopher called.

It felt exquisitely bold to let this startling version of herself step out of that changeroom.

Christopher stepped back and tapped his chin, assessing, but it was Liam she was watching. He looked up from his phone and his mouth fell open.

The look on his face both thrilled her and terrified her.

A boss couldn't look at an employee like that! It was the precise reason she'd been dressing down for months.

Because that look—that she probably would secretly revisit for the rest of her life—could cause complications of the worst kind in the workplace. It was the kind of look that could make a woman hope for things she could never have.

Still, a part of her that was not rational gloried in his gaze.

A man's frank appreciation of a woman.

But rational had always saved her, and while she could enjoy this moment, her enjoyment had to be brief. She couldn't live in a place like this and maintain the most important thing of all.

Control.

Liam seemed to reach the exact same conclusion because he snapped his mouth shut and looked back at his phone. "You dress up pretty good, Sunday."

"Thanks, chief."

"The Oscars, yes," Christopher decided with a

reluctant sigh, "an awards banquet, even an upscale one, no."

And so Molly's moment as Cinderella drew to a reluctant—but blessed—close.

She went back into the cubicle and took off the dress. She put on the final choice, Liam's pick.

When she turned to face herself in the mirror, she was shocked to see Liam's choice for her was even more stunning than the Cinderella gown had been. Because the dress that had looked uninteresting, possibly even dowdy, on the hanger, looked incredible on.

It was the simplest of dresses, a sleeveless sheath. There was no plunging neckline and it ended modestly just above her knee.

And yet it was a dress that celebrated sensuality, but ever so subtly. It was sophisticated, and made her feel exquisitely—and powerfully—feminine.

She took a deep breath. There it was again. She could taste it on the air.

Change, a storm at its beginning stages, when it could seem so benign, even exhilarating.

She stepped out of the change room and avoided Liam's gaze. Christopher nodded his approval. "Obviously, the one. Let me go find shoes and accessories to match."

He was gone in a flash, but the truth was she had barely registered him.

She finally built up her nerve enough to meet Liam's eyes. There was that look again, even more intense than it had been with the bronze dress. It was a look that could melt bones. He masked it quickly, looked back at his phone again.

"You look great, Sunday," he offered, the faintest hoarse note in his voice.

Christopher was back. He set impossibly high heels on the floor in front of her and secured a simple strand of pearls around her neck.

She stepped into the shoes, and Christopher sighed with satisfaction.

"Perfect," he breathed. "Classic. Audrey Hepburn, *Breakfast at Tiffany's*. Well, almost perfect. The hair! Have we got time for a quick visit to the salon side?"

She glanced at her watch. "Fifty-one minutes," she said to Liam. "Forty-one, if we arrive ten minutes early."

He lifted a shoulder. "Or forty-six if we arrive five minutes early."

The best possible thing happened. Their eyes met. She felt the way she felt in the office. Connected. On the same page. A team with common goals and a common understanding of how they would arrive at them.

They laughed.

Christopher whisked her quickly to the salon side.

A stylist, Ramone, freed her hair from the bun that was much the worse for wear for all the dresses being pulled on and off over her head.

"Oh, my," he said. "Why would you wear all this glorious hair like that? I don't have time to cut it, much as I would like to. I'll just quickly style it. I don't even need the iron."

He took Molly's hair and wound it around his fingers, fluffing and spraying as he went.

The result was an extraordinary cascade of big looping curls.

"Give your head a shake," the stylist said.

It took Molly a full second to realize he meant it literally. She shook her head, and her hair swayed and danced in a sensuous wave before falling naturally to the curve of her shoulders.

Hair completed, the stylist opened brand-new makeup packets and continued to work. Molly really did need to give her head a shake at what was emerging. Her cheeks looked sculpted.

And her lips! They looked full and faintly pouty…and like lips that invited kisses.

"Close your eyes," Ramone said. "Last thing. There. Presto, done."

Molly reached for her glasses.

"You are not putting those back on! They fall in the same category as the way you wear your hair. As in, why?" The stylist set them playfully on the end of his own nose, and his expression became bewildered.

"They're not even prescription!" he said, accusingly. "You don't need glasses!"

He looked as if he was going to toss them out, but Molly rescued them.

"Why?" the stylist asked her again.

"Because I want to be taken seriously," Molly

said, defensively. "I want to look like a professional. Not like—"

She stared at her reflection in the mirror.

"A supermodel?" Ramone suggested.

"What have you done to my eyes?"

Her eyes suddenly seemed to take up her whole face. They looked huge and a turquoise shade had emerged in them.

"Just added a little something. Your natural lash is great, but everybody can benefit from a little enhancement."

In the life-is-full-of-surprises department Molly would have never guessed she would be wearing false eyelashes by the end of the day.

Or that she'd like them!

She reminded herself, but without too much sincerity, that she didn't like surprises.

She really did look like a supermodel. She really did need to give her head a shake now!

In fact, a stranger looked back at her. An utterly gorgeous stranger.

Should she ask Ramone to tone it down? She didn't feel like herself. She felt like she was pretending to be someone else.

But really? There was no time now for a redo, and in a way she *was* pretending to be someone else.

"Embrace it," Ramone said, softly, as if Molly had spoken all her doubts out loud.

Why not follow that well-meaning advice? Why

not embrace this alter ego, this hidden side of herself; why not give herself the freedom to play with it?

Why not brush off that sense of *not good enough* that clung to her like a greasy scent of cooking that had gotten into her clothes?

She was pretending tonight, anyway. She was pretending to be Liam's plus-one. She was always way too serious. Why not, for once in her life, have fun with it? Why not embrace it? Why not dance with it?

Just until the clock struck midnight?

What harm could come from it? Just once. It occurred to Molly that was very likely what everybody who played with matches said.

CHAPTER SIX

MOLLY GLANCED AT her watch.

Christopher appeared at her side, made a face at the watch, whisked it from her wrist and put it in the black clutch that he handed her. He pried the glasses from her grip and put those in the bag, too. Then, he helped her out of Ramone's salon chair and pushed her gently toward the front lobby where Liam was waiting, looking out the front window, rocking back on his heels.

"We have two minutes to be five minutes early," he said, and then turned to look at her.

For a moment, he looked utterly stunned, his composure completely gone. She had not been aware that some of his suave confidence was a mask, until it slipped.

And what she saw underneath it was even more compelling.

One hundred percent pure man.

Something powerful, raw and vulnerable at the same time in his face.

"Sunday," he finally asked. "Is that you?"

"To be perfectly honest, I'm not sure."

"What did you do to your hair?" he croaked.

"Oh—" she touched it self-consciously "—it's just down."

"What happened to your eyes?"

"False lashes. I believe the legs of a thousand spiders were harvested to create this look, so I hope you appreciate their sacrifice, poor things."

He smiled at that.

She opened up the handbag Christopher had given her, and took out the eyeglasses. She settled them on her face. Even if they weren't real, she felt so much better wearing them. The fake glasses made her feel as if she was herself.

"Whew," he said. "You are *my* Sunday. I think. I have to make absolutely sure."

She cocked her head at him.

"What's the capital of Bolivia?"

"It actually has two capitals. La Paz is the administrative capital, while Sucre is the constitutional capital."

His smile deepened, and somehow they moved closer to what they really were, as the unguarded expression left his face.

"Um, boss, we have to run," she said, peering in her purse at her confiscated watch. "We literally now have one minute to be five minutes early."

"Maybe for tonight," he said, "you should call me Liam."

"All right," she said, and then after hesitating just a second, "Liam."

She couldn't believe the way his name came off her lips. Good grief. All husky and sensual, somehow.

Despite the fact they were running late, they both stood there for a moment, contemplating how such a small thing felt like a momentous shift.

But then *her* Liam was back. Despite her using his first name, one hundred percent her boss.

Confident.

Suave.

In control.

But once you had caught a glimpse of the other, could you ever forget it?

"Can you run in those shoes?" he asked her.

"I doubt it," she said.

And just like that his hand was in hers, and they were running out onto Fifth Avenue, dodging through an indulgent early evening crowd, sharing laughter over her absolute clumsiness in the unfamiliar shoes.

They arrived, breathless, at the venue. Liam let go of Molly's hand.

Her hand in his, as they had navigated the crowds, was even more unsettling than her amazing transformation. If he resisted looking at her, though, which was difficult, and didn't take her hand again, it was going to be much easier to think of her as his always faithful assistant, just filling in, helping him out for the evening.

A single photographer stood outside the venue, glancing moodily at the sky. Liam followed his gaze and realized it looked as if it might rain. The front steps were completely empty, which reminded him they were running late. The attendees were all already inside.

"Not much of a turnout from the press corps," he said to the photographer, who lifted his camera to his eye in a rather desultory way and took their picture. He surveyed the result in the window at the back of the camera and then tucked the camera in his bag.

"Innovators on the Move?" he said, dismissively. "Nonevent. Except for Eva La Lydia. She sent out a blanket text saying she'd had a last-minute change of plans. I'm sure there's a swarm outside Lucali's at the moment. She hinted Douglas Hampton might be with her."

"Oh," Molly murmured. "Good old garlic breath."

"I mean, sorry, Mr. Westerhouse," the photographer said, "but that trumps a two-years-ago 'Bachelor of the Year.'"

"Ah," Liam said. Despite the missed publicity opportunity for both the Innovators and FIX, his relief at not being with Miss La Lydia was immense. He hadn't liked the fact she'd been rude to Molly and he liked her even less now that he knew she kept the paparazzi on speed dial.

"Why did you stay?" he asked the photographer.

A lifted shoulder. "Always the chance of getting the surprise shot. Or scoop. Who are you?" the photographer asked Molly, looking at her with sudden and faintly predatory interest, as if she might be that scoop.

Liam actually felt Molly shrink beside him. There was that deer-in-the-headlights look again. He nodded at the photographer, put his hand on the small of Molly's back and guided her into the safety of the building.

Inside, particularly once they'd been shown to their seats, Molly relaxed and looked around with that curiosity that was inherent to her.

He appreciated Molly even more as the evening went on. Because, while some people would find the awards part of the function exceedingly dull, she did not. At one point, she leaned over and asked him for his phone.

"I accidentally left mine at Second Chances," she whispered.

He unlocked his phone and handed it to her unhesitatingly, which he realized was an unconscious measure of his trust in her.

She opened an app, and when he glanced over, he was very relieved to see that despite the startling new look, there was *his* Sunday, totally engrossed in making notes about people being given awards, and the products or techniques they had developed.

Again, Liam was grateful Eva was not here. Even knowing next to nothing about her, he was familiar with the type. He suspected by now she would have been fidgeting in her seat and plotting how to draw attention to herself.

He got up and gave the award, and when he came back to his seat Molly was beaming at him.

"That was amazing," she said. "You hit all the right notes. Look at Jordan! She's just so happy."

He was a successful man. He received awards and accolades and attention all the time.

Why did the look on Molly's face eclipse all of those?

Because in a world where you could not trust much, and where things did not always end up being as they appeared, his Woman Sunday was one hundred percent authentic. Which was ironic, given that she was *pretending* to be his date tonight.

"You want to get out of here?" he asked her when the awards show drew to a close. There was a cocktail meet and greet after, but it occurred to him he'd imposed on his assistant quite enough for one day.

"Oh, no," she said. "I think you should go talk to Jordan." She still had his phone. She consulted her notes. "And I want to talk to James McPherson about his hydrogen energy research. And also Lucy Williams about that camera she developed. I hope she has a prototype with her."

Despite how glamorous she looked, Liam was inordinately relieved that this definitely was his Sunday: earnest, enthusiastic, serious, all business.

"Can I get you a drink?" he asked. "Wine? Cocktail?"

"Oh," she said, and something flashed in her face that he didn't quite understand. "I don't drink."

"Not at all?" He had thought a bit of alcohol might help her relax in this new environment.

"Well," she laughed uncomfortably. "You know. Water."

Always so literal, dotting every *i* and crossing every *t*, making sure there were no misunderstandings.

"I meant alcohol," he clarified.

Again, that look on her face. He was momentarily reminded that there were many things about Molly Littleton that he didn't know.

"Oh," she said, her light tone not matching the look in her eyes. "I've just never seen anything good come out of it."

He cocked his head at her, intrigued. First of all, he could hear the accent he had never noticed before. Barely, but there. And like the barely discernable accent, this disclosure hinted that his straightlaced assistant had experienced a life he knew nothing about. Was that deliberate on her part? Or a lack of interest on his?

A healthy lack of interest, he told himself sternly; he did not *need* to know a single thing about Molly Littleton's personal life.

And yet, still, he probed, tentatively, keeping his tone deliberately light. "What does that mean? Spiked punch at the high school prom?"

"Exactly!" she said.

He felt the oddest little shiver along his spine. His one hundred percent trustworthy assistant had just lied to him.

Her eyes lit up. "Look. It's Frank Beltane. He's the one who has that idea about the dog-walking apparatus."

And just like that, she was gone.

Had she really been that enthused about spotting Frank? Or had she literally stepped away from the conversation?

He watched her get Frank's attention, watched the man's face light up at being buttonholed by such a beautiful woman, but then, within seconds they were engrossed in an earnest conversation, as if they had known each other for years, not seconds.

His discomfort over her lying to him eased. He could be wrong, after all. He was seeing her in a new way, and it might have made him extrasensitive to nuances he'd never noticed before.

Or maybe she'd had—as had most people—a terrible experience with drinking. Who wanted to tell their boss about ending up in a bad situation because of inexperience and bad choices brought on by drinking?

Though it must have been very bad for her to never drink again.

Making way too big a deal of it, Liam told himself, and deliberately rolled his shoulders to release some unexpected tension from them.

Possibly bringing his own bad experiences to the table.

He'd nearly gotten married once, to a woman who was not one single thing that she had claimed to be or that he had thought she was. He could still feel the wound of it.

That was what had made him hypersensitive to the possibility Molly had lied to him. His own baggage, not hers.

And really, wasn't all his baggage what made Molly the perfect companion for the evening?

It was *never* going anywhere. She was too valuable an assistant—the best he'd ever had—to risk it all going down the tubes over the fact he'd noticed tonight she was beautiful as well as extraordinary at her job.

CHAPTER SEVEN

LIAM WAS SOON surrounded by people wanting his attention, and he turned his energy, deliberately, to that, listening, asking questions about ideas, digging deeper. This was at the heart of everything he did: digging through mountains of coal for the diamonds he knew were there.

Still, he was aware his legendary focus was just a touch off. As the evening went on, Liam was constantly keeping track of Molly, watching her out of the corner of his eye, seeing how people reacted to her.

Considering her initial discomfort when they had gone to Second Chances, he had expected she might be a little more clingy, but she had found her groove, and he dismissed any remaining niggles of apprehension he'd felt earlier. Watching her interact with people, Liam felt newly appreciative of how lucky he was to have her.

And yet by the end of the evening, that appreciation was faintly tinged with something darker. Molly had an absolute swarm of young men around her.

It isn't jealousy, he told himself sternly.

Worry, maybe. Professional. That someone would spot her spellbinding combination of brilliance and efficiency and try to steal her from him.

But no, that wasn't it. Not exactly.

He realized he felt protective of her. Molly was indeed smart and efficient, but there was also a naivete about her that was in stark contrast to the sophistication of New York.

Again, it was that side of her he hadn't noticed before. In the office, a very contained environment, that didn't show at all.

But in that dress shop, it had been so apparent that she was a duck out of water and that her strengths in the office didn't really transfer to other worlds. He was keeping a sharp eye on her because he didn't want her to get bowled over by her popularity. Be taken advantage of.

You're such a hero, he chided himself, as he went and rescued Molly from a young innovator who was getting way too close to her.

"I think it's time to go," he told her.

He saw the relief in her eyes, the flash of annoyance in the slightly inebriated young man's. Liam raised an eyebrow at him that sent him scuttling off for cover.

It took a while to leave—stopped so many times on the way—but finally, they made it to the door.

As they left the building, the storm that had threatened earlier had broken. They stood under an overhang at the front door watching water sluice off the roof.

"You seemed to really fit in," he ventured, peering out at the rain.

"Oh," she said, with a happy laugh, "it was like a nerd convention. Of course I fit in. But I have to say, my feet are killing me."

And then she bent over and slipped off the shoes, dangling them in her hand and squinting at the sky. "I'm going to make a dash for it, boss."

"A dash for it? In your bare feet? And where do you think you're going?"

"I'll grab the subway. Of course, not in my bare feet. What do you think I am, a hillbilly?"

For a moment she looked as if she wanted to clap her hand over her mouth, but instead she bent and put the shoes back on, wincing as she straightened.

"I don't care how much you love the subway," he told her firmly, "you are not taking it home at this time of night, dressed like that. You'd be soaked before you got across the street."

She glanced down at herself as if she'd forgotten, totally, how she was dressed.

"Fine," she said. "I'll call a rideshare."

"I'm calling the car for you."

"It's nearly midnight. Don't get Paul out of bed. I'm comfortable with the rideshare."

He wasn't. But how far did he push the protector thing without seeming overbearing and as if he did not trust her competence?

But then she stared down at the bag she was carrying and frowned.

"I just remembered, I don't have my phone. Can I borrow yours again?"

And then the frown morphed into total alarm.

"What?" he asked.

"I don't have my purse," she stammered. "I just have this one Christopher gave me. It's not just my phone. I don't have any money—or my credit card—to pay a rideshare."

"Oh, for pity's sake, Sunday. Do you think I wouldn't pay for you to get home?"

He looked at her outfit. Despite the fact they were standing in the scant protection of the overhang, it seemed to be reacting to the dampness in the air, clinging to her.

He was distressed to notice how his assistant was quite curvy.

And her luscious hair, beginning to curl wildly about her face, was very sexy.

He wasn't putting her in a rideshare or a cab.

"I think the best thing would be to call Paul, after all," he said.

"Yes, I think that would be best," she said. "Thank you."

But before he could fish his phone out of his pocket, she closed her eyes, rocked back on her heels and groaned.

"Feet?" he asked, sympathetically.

"Worse. Boss, I don't have anything from my purse, including my house keys."

He let that sink in. "Do you want me to get you a hotel room for the night?"

"You know I'm something of an expert at booking hotel rooms, right?"

"I hadn't thought of it, but now that you point it out, it's part of what you do to make my life so seamless, isn't it?"

"It is," she said, sadly. "And this is what I know about hotels: Without ID it would be easier to get into Buckingham Palace or Fort Knox than to get a hotel room."

"But surely if I go in with you—"

She shook her head, and her hair cascaded down around her shoulders. He knew it would be the wrong time to laugh at her dilemmas and he tried to stifle his smile, but she squinted at him dangerously.

"Is there something about the fact I'm going to be sleeping in an alley tonight that you find amusing?"

"Well, you have to see the irony. The woman I count on to fix *everything* has been given an unfixable problem of her own."

"Oh, yes, very funny. Ha ha."

He couldn't help but notice she was starting to shiver.

"You know, even though I've come to count on you to solve every problem and it's probably made me quite lazy, I can still pull a solution to a dilemma out of the hat when I have to."

"And? Your solution?"

"You'll come home with me, of course."

It was a humiliating ending to what had been such a good evening. Pretending to be Liam's plus-one had not been nearly as challenging as Molly had thought it was going to be. After her initial discomfort in the dress store, it had really been quite fun, and certainly stimulating.

She had learned a great deal on topics she had known nothing about previously, and she always enjoyed that. It had been like gathering information at a living library tonight.

Molly *loved* learning. She loved that black-and-white world. She liked adding to the formidable arsenal that her brain kept of *facts*, those wonderful immutable things that did not have any kind of emotional complexity attached to them.

Not like being asked why you didn't drink.

Not like being invited home with her boss. A dumb mistake had put her in a very awkward predicament.

It grated on the perfectionist in her. She was a detail person. She could ferret out the potential for disaster, for every single thing that could go wrong; she prided herself on putting out fires before they started.

Except, as Liam had pointed out, just a little too gleefully, in her own life.

"Don't worry," he said, "there's nothing inappropriate about it. I host guests all the time."

She *knew* that, because she was the juggler who kept all the balls in the air.

"You know Maria and Paul have a suite in my apartment."

Of course they did. She knew that. She knew he

had staff live with him. She often liaised with both Maria and Paul on logistical matters: deliveries, dinner guests, overnight stays, transport.

"So, we'll be chaperoned," he said. And then laughed again. "A chaperoned charade."

"Don't be ridiculous," she snapped at him. "We don't need a chaperone. I trust you completely."

His eyes flitted to her hair, and then her lips. Finally, he met her eyes. "Good," he said, a little hoarsely.

"It's just awkward."

"Ah well, really, Sunday? What's life without the odd little surprise thrown in?"

Stable, she thought, *safe*.

And maybe just a little bit dull. She sighed. "Thank you for your generous invitation. I have no choice but to accept."

"Gracious," he said.

"Nothing personal. Just caught out."

"The thing you like the least. The rain's letting up a bit. Should we walk, or should I call Paul?"

It would be utterly ridiculous to call Paul. They could walk to his apartment before the poor man got out of bed.

"Walk," she said.

Unfortunately, every step was pain. Though she tried bravely to hide it, Liam noticed, stopped and guided her to a step they were passing by.

"Sit down."

Was he going to call Paul after all? So silly, only

a few more blocks. Still, she was not sure how she could make it.

He crouched in front of her and slipped one shoe off her aching foot. She looked at the top of his head, and had a sudden irresistible desire to touch those tawny locks. She tucked her errant hands under her thighs.

"Sunday," he said, unaware of the terrible battle being waged within her, "you've got a really bad blister on the back of your heel. The strap must have been rubbing."

It was a sign of a life bereft of human touch that his hand felt so blissful cupping her foot. She pulled her foot away hastily. She didn't want him to notice her rough, calloused soles.

"I don't like my feet being touched."

He lifted an eyebrow. "Ticklish?"

She'd let him think what he wanted.

He slid off her other shoe. "I'll just look," he assured her. "This foot has a blister, too, only it's right here."

Despite his promise not to touch, his finger gently stroked a raw place on the side of her big toe.

The combination of pleasure and pain made her draw in her breath.

"I'll go barefoot the rest of the way," she offered, quickly, drawing her foot out of his hand. *Like a hillbilly.* She didn't say it out loud this time, though.

"You're not going barefoot in New York City!" he said.

A *hillbilly* who hadn't worn a real pair of shoes

until she was six years old. And then, they were only for school, not to be worn casually.

When she went to the spa now, the pedicurists almost always gathered wide-eyed around her feet, chatting among themselves in a different language.

But you didn't have to speak their language to know that no amount of emery boarding could fix that! Her hardscrabble previous life was etched into the hardened soles and thick calluses on her feet. New York City was nothing compared to places where she had dug her toes into Red River dirt.

Unfortunately, while the soles of her feet were as tough as shoe leather, the rest of them, unusually wide because of her early shoelessness, didn't fit most real girl shoes.

Liam still crouched in front of her, turned now, his back to her.

"It's only a few blocks," he said, and reached around and patted his back invitingly. "Hop on."

Her boss was going to piggyback her through the streets of New York? Of course she had to say no. She had to suck it up and put those shoes back on.

It was so unprofessional!

And so sweet.

In fact, it was entirely and utterly irresistible.

Still gripping her shoes by their straps in one hand and her purse in the other, Molly stood up behind him and put her palms on his shoulders. She could feel the springy strength of his muscles, the beautiful broadness of him underneath the custom tailoring of his jacket. Hesitantly, one at a time,

Molly slid her legs around his waist and put her arms around his neck, her shoes and purse dangling under his chin. Her dress hiked up past her thighs.

His arms locked behind him, supporting her bottom, and he eased to his feet. The rain was a bit harder, now, but she could feel the heat rising off his back, scorching her inner thighs.

That hair that she had wanted so badly to touch was tickling at her face, and the damp was releasing a scent from it that was as crisp and clean as freshly laundered linens.

The rain started with a vengeance then, and he snugged her in tight to his back and stepped forward. His strength was easy and unselfconscious. After a moment, juggling her weight while she soaked up the unexpected and sweet ecstasy of this physical closeness, he broke into an easy lope.

"If you want to go faster," he said. "You don't have to slap me in the face with your shoes and purse—the more traditional *giddyap* will do."

She tightened her grip, but the shoes were still bouncing around, and he exaggerated his head bob, pretending to dodge them, and yelling, "Ow," every time one grazed him.

"Giddyap," she said, feeling crazily inebriated, as if she had imbibed after all. She swatted him with her purse, and he complied with a surge of speed.

Molly began to laugh at the total wonderful absurdity of what was happening. And the absolute unexpected intimacy of it, too.

At this moment in time, they were not a boss and his assistant.

Not the CEO and his plus-one.

Nothing about this felt like a charade. In fact, it felt like one of the most real things she had ever experienced.

They felt like any normal guy and his girl caught in a rainstorm in New York City.

His laughter, deep, rumbling, a total letting go, joined hers.

And then they were charging together through a New York night, dodging in and out of late-night pedestrians, and through puddles and across streets, the peals of their laughter a private delight in a public world.

Molly felt something in her, always tightly wound, always in control, let go, completely, wildly, ecstatically, as she clung to Liam tighter.

As she surrendered, it felt as if his strength, and his aroma, filled every part of her, parts that she hadn't known were empty.

She wondered, ever so briefly, if it spoke to a life devoid of even simple pleasures, that this moment had a peculiar shine to it.

That it rose easily to the top of the best moments of her entire life.

CHAPTER EIGHT

Liam set Molly down on the sidewalk in front of his building. Molly was soaked. Her glasses were so wet that looking through them gave the sense the world had turned into a large impressionist piece of art, all the lines and colors wavering and blurred, utterly vibrant.

Her dress clung stubbornly, stuck to her thigh where it had ridden up when she had accepted that invitation to climb on his back. She was trying to yank it down when he turned to face her.

Molly straightened, and drank in the sight of him. Like her, he was utterly soaked, his jacket and slacks clinging to him, his shirt nearly transparent. She could make out the hard lines of his chest and belly underneath it, even the dark circle of his nipple.

He was the one who had been running, carrying her; he should have been the one who was red-faced and breathless.

But it was she who could barely breathe, who could feel her heart threatening to leave the confines of her chest. Her thighs, the only dry place on her, were burning from the heat of such intimate contact with him. It felt as if they might burst into flame.

"Cold?" he asked when she shivered. He took her arm, and guided her up a few wide, shallow steps to the protection of the portico around the entrance to his building.

She was about as far from cold as you could get. On the other hand, Liam was smiling easily, his eyes still holding the spark of the laughter they'd just shared.

He didn't look at all how she felt, which was entirely discombobulated.

In fact, he looked as if he piggybacked women through the rain-soaked streets of New York at a casual lope every day of his life.

His hair was wet to the scalp, slicked to his head, and it had turned a darker shade of gold. She watched a raindrop—or maybe a single bead of sweat—slide out from under a lock of that hair, run down his temple, over his cheek and then zigzag crazily toward his lip.

She stared as that drop found his upper lip, and his tongue reached out and flicked it.

As it turned out, she hadn't been as far from cold as you could get. There had been some wiggle room, because she felt a bolt of heat run through her that felt as if she had been struck by lightning.

He reached, casually, for her glasses, and slid them off her nose. Wordlessly, he slipped a corner of his shirt out from under his waistband—

the only part of him that was dry—and wiped the water from her lenses, before he carefully placed them back on her nose.

It was a good thing she was so wet, or she was pretty sure she would have spontaneously ignited. It probably spoke to a very pathetic life that it was just about the most romantic thing that had ever happened to her.

She turned away from him hastily, and made a pretense of studying his building.

It was right across the street from the south end of Central Park, and even a relative newcomer to New York, like her, knew this was the toniest address in a city of very posh addresses. This historic sandstone building was iconic. A rare apartment had come available in this building a few days ago and been snatched up. It had made the news for breaking New York's record per-square-foot price.

"Come on," he said. "Let's get in before you shiver to death."

A uniformed doorman appeared and held open the door for them.

"Mr. Westerhouse. Miss."

Not a ripple of *anything* in that man's face that hinted if there was anything unusual about Liam showing up with a barefoot girl on his back at nearly midnight, both of them soaked to the skin.

"Thanks, Mike," he said to the doorman. "Have you had a good night?"

She had always liked this about Liam. No matter who he encountered, he had that gift for making them feel seen and appreciated.

She needed to remind herself of that. It was the way he was in the world. From acknowledging the doorman to wiping water off a pair of eyeglasses, it wasn't *personal*. He was naturally considerate. It would be a terrible invitation to disappointment to take it any other way.

Liam led her through the lobby, and the feeling Molly had had of being deeply connected to him fled. She was very aware of the differences in their worlds as she tried not to gawk at everything.

She kept her mouth firmly shut, but the entrance area was utterly spectacular, with huge, crystal-dripping chandeliers dropping from an intricately patterned plastered ceiling. Hardwood, laid in herringbone, was covered with gorgeous area rugs. Deep couches faced each other, with a backdrop of huge arched windows that looked out toward Central Park on one side of them, and a huge gas fireplace, lit, on the other.

It looked like she imagined a living room in a palace would look.

"Does anyone ever actually sit here?" she whispered, awed.

Liam looked at the area as if he'd never noticed it before.

"What would they do here?" she asked. "I mean it looks as if it would be a very nice place to spend an afternoon with a book, except it's a little public. I mean, don't they have their own apartments for that?"

He looked amused by her, and she felt gauche.

"It would be a beautiful place for a wedding reception."

Now why had she said that? And why had she sounded so wistful, getting "hickier" by the moment.

"I think people just wait here. Like to meet friends or to wait for a car. I'll pay more attention and report back to you, Sunday."

"Thank you," she said, solemnly. She begged herself to stop digging in deeper, but she had to add, a little primly, "Because that seems like an extravagant waste of very expensive real estate."

He laughed then. "A missed opportunity for building income," he said. He was teasing her, but it made her acutely aware this world was as foreign to her as the face of the moon.

At the elevator bank, she looked back and saw the prints of her wet bare feet tracking across the shiny floor, next to his shoe prints.

Did someone come behind her and clean that up?

Liam was untroubled by such questions, apparently. He slid a card from his pocket and tapped it against a wall-mounted keypad. The doors instantly whispered open.

"Good timing," she said. "Just as if it was waiting for us."

"It was," he said, as they stepped inside. "It's private. It only goes to my floor."

A private elevator, one they were dripping puddles of water in. Again, he seemed untroubled, while she fought an urge to find a rag or a paper towel and look after it. The rich scent of wood polish came off the glossy walls and combined with the rich aromas of him.

Her feeling of being in a movie, or a dream, only intensified as the elevator doors whispered open again at *his* floor.

Nothing in her whole life—not even the rich, subtle, tasteful decor at the office, or the palace-style ambience of the lobby—could have prepared her for the exquisite poshness of his apartment.

With a tilt of his head and a gesture with his arm, he invited her to step out of the elevator ahead of him. She found herself in a wide entry mezzanine, the marble floor deliciously cold and smooth beneath her bare feet. She avoided creating a puddle on a subtly faded rug with deep colors and an intricate tapestry pattern that looked as if it belonged on a wall in a museum, not on a floor.

She could see the mezzanine opened up to a living room, softly lit, even though no one was in it. Banks of windows faced the darkened park, and two exquisite sofas faced each other over a coffee table that held a stunning bronze sculpture. At odds with the ultrasleek, sophisticated decor, somehow the piece, a cowboy on a horse, couldn't have been more perfect.

Molly was aware of feeling one hundred percent paralyzed as Liam pried her hands off her shoes, glared at them for a minute, and then put them, with a touch of ceremony, in an empty wastebasket under an antique entry table.

"I think those cost the earth," she said, uneasily.

"It doesn't matter what they cost," he said. "It matters what they're worth. Which is zero, given the injury they've caused you."

"Still," she said. "Maybe a secondhand store?"

"What kind of person are you? Would you really inflict that kind of misery on someone else?"

Then, discussion over, he tossed his elevator card on the entry table, stripped off his coat, threw it on an upholstered bench.

Her focus shifted off the shoes. Was she going to go into that gorgeous room? With this gorgeous man whose shirt was sticking to him? And then what? She could stare at him admiringly while they soaked—and possibly ruined—the buttery leather of those couches?

"I don't have anything to change into," she realized out loud. "And no pajamas, no toiletries. Nothing to wear tomorrow."

She looked down at her soaked dress glumly. She wondered if the beautiful garment was completely ruined. She looked back at Liam, who cocked his head at her, registering her discomfort.

"Normally, I have this amazing assistant who could solve all that in a—" he said, and snapped his fingers.

He was trying to put her at ease.

She was fighting a desire to bolt.

And then a woman, graying hair, in a neat bun, and a sturdy skirt and matching blouse, came around the corner.

"Luckily," he said, smiling, "we have Maria, who is nearly as good as you at solving problems and putting out fires. Molly, Maria. Maria, Molly."

Molly felt relief surge through her as Maria came and took her hand.

"Finally, we meet Miss Sunday," Maria said.

Of course, Molly had dealt with Maria many times, though they had not met yet.

Maria was to Liam's personal life what Molly was to his professional one.

Her relief, she realized, was mostly because of Maria's innate warmth. It was like being greeted at the door by a beloved grandmother.

It eased some of her sense of being somewhere that she didn't belong. That she would never belong.

"Molly finds herself without her house keys—" Liam filled Maria in "—so she'll be staying the night. She doesn't have, um…anything."

"Come with me," Maria said, and Molly found herself being led in the direction Maria had come from.

Again, she tried not to gawk at the gorgeous paintings and decor in the wide hallway.

Just past a state-of-the-art kitchen, Maria opened a door to a room, and Molly went in to find herself in an opulent guest suite.

"The bathroom is through there," Maria said. "Have a quick hot shower. It will take the chill off. There's a robe on the back of the door. Come out to the kitchen when you're done. I'll have hot chocolate."

Molly thought she should refuse, that she shouldn't impose on the hospitality of Liam and his staff any more than she had to.

It was so late. Maria probably would like to go to bed, though there had not been a flicker of anything but welcome in her lovely crinkled face.

On the other hand, Molly was here. She was probably going to be in a situation like this once in her entire life.

Why spoil it? Why not just enjoy it all as the spectacular, unexpected gift that it was?

"Hot chocolate sounds amazing," she said. And it did.

Speaking of amazing, that also described the suite she found herself in. It was stunning with its huge bed, tone on tone decor and wall-to-wall windows that looked out over the skyline of the city.

She wanted to go look out that window, but she was aware she was dripping onto the thick carpet, and suddenly a shower felt like the best idea ever.

The water pounding down on her rain-chilled flesh was just what she needed. She stepped out of it, finally, when she realized the hot water was *never* running out. She found a robe—luxuriously thick and pristinely white, as if it was brand-new—on a hook behind the door. She pulled it on, and then towel-dried her hair, squeezing the water from it.

A bit self-consciously, she stepped out into the

hallway and made her way to the kitchen. Somehow, she had thought she was going to be alone with Maria there, but Liam was there already, sitting at a small kitchen table, talking animatedly with the older woman.

His freshly showered aroma filled her nostrils. He had on a T-shirt and a pair of string-tied pants. It was the most casual she had ever seen him. She tried not to stare at his arms. She'd only seen him in long sleeves previously, sometimes rolled up at the cuff.

Seeing the lovely bulge of his biceps made her think what a shame it was to keep those arms covered up!

Coupled with the fact she was in a housecoat, the moment was infused with an intimacy just as powerful as riding on his back had been. She was not sure how much more she could handle of her boss tonight!

"Actually, I'm going to bow out of the hot chocolate—"

"Nonsense," he said. "Sunday! You haven't lived until you've had Maria's hot chocolate. Plus, I was just bragging you up. Maria. Ask her anything."

Maria came and put a thick mug on the table. Steam rose from it, and it was topped with a mound of thick cream and chocolate shavings. The aroma was an enchantment.

Molly was drawn to that table like a magnet being drawn to steel.

"Some cooks use a secret ingredient in apple pie," Maria said. "Do you know what it is?"

Molly took a sip of the hot chocolate. She closed her eyes. "Ambrosia," she said.

"Well, I do like a good Ambrosia apple for pie, but that wasn't what I meant."

"Oh, and I was referring to the hot chocolate. Ambrosia are known to be good pie apples, because they're so sweet and hold their shape while cooking. Their lower acidity can mean less sugar is needed."

"You bake!" Maria said, as if this was an accomplishment equivalent to a moonwalk.

"Oh, no, sorry, I didn't mean to give that impression. I read a story once called 'Apple of My Eye,' and some of the details stuck."

"Ah," Maria said, clearly not seeing reading as quite the same kind of accomplishment as baking.

"Anyway, I think occasionally amaretto or rum are considered a secret ingredient—flavor enhancers—in apple pie."

Maria went back to looking impressed. "Spaghetti?"

"Sometimes cinnamon."

Liam lifted a shoulder and grinned. "Told you."

Maria shot Liam a look, patted Molly's shoulder and then left them alone.

Alone.

"Hey," Liam said. "Do you want to take this out on the deck?"

A deck in New York City. In a housecoat. With

the world's best hot chocolate and the world's best-looking man, who was unselfconsciously showing off his unexpectedly lovely arms.

Tomorrow she could let her life get back to normal.

Tonight she was embracing every sweet surprise that life gave her. She followed Liam through his extraordinary living room and a patio door that slid silently open to the deck.

Decks were rare enough in New York City, but this one was huge, its flagstones wet and shiny, the rain bouncing off them.

But they didn't even get wet, as there were deeply cushioned lounge chairs under a roofed pagoda structure.

She settled into the chair, her feet stretched out before her. She pulled the housecoat belt tight around her. Her every sense seemed to be extraordinarily heightened. She took a sip of the hot chocolate and closed her eyes.

"I *love* Maria," she said. What she really meant was that she loved it all.

"She was in charge of the school kitchen at my private school, and Paul was in charge of the garages."

He hesitated, and Molly held her breath, turning slightly to look at him.

He looked unusually pensive, not the laughing man who had carried her through the rain-washed streets.

Something different was happening here. It was

evident from his silence and his facial expression—Liam was debating something.

"They saved me," he said, quietly.

Molly could feel something exquisite unfolding inside her. *This*, this moment felt like they were moving into new territory. He'd alluded earlier today about an unhappy childhood and now it seemed he was going to say more.

She felt the trust in the confidence he had just shared with her, and his trust felt as much a gift—maybe more so—than everything else that had happened tonight, including the surprise piggyback ride.

CHAPTER NINE

Liam didn't know why he had said that.

He and Molly had an astounding working relationship, but before today, he rarely revealed anything about his personal life.

Why would he jeopardize what they had by introducing new elements? He could feel the vulnerability in it.

He ordered himself to back up, to back away. He was under the spell of something and he needed to break out of it.

But he didn't. His legendary discipline failed him. He *wanted* her to know this other side of him. He felt compelled to tell her.

Well, if you were going to tell anyone, why not Molly? She radiated trustworthiness. Even now, she didn't press, at all. Waited. Silently. A promise of some kind of acceptance of him in that silence that he could not resist.

"Even before I went to private school, I'd found my way to the kitchens and garages of the various places we called home, though I use the term loosely. None of them were actually *homey.*

"Except in the kitchens and the staff quarters, the garages. There was warmth there that I craved. All the staff always made a fuss over me. When I started tinkering with mechanical things, I got a lot of approval for it.

"Maybe the first approval of my life. I don't actually know why my parents had a child," he said, slowly. "They both seemed equally baffled by this small, noisy, energetic creature in their household. I didn't really fit into their lifestyle. They off-loaded caring about me. There were nannies, and it seemed as soon as it was a possibility, off to private school I went.

"I didn't fit in at private school any better than I had at home. I wasn't interested in the things that interested my schoolmates, especially sports. I was intensely interested in how things work. And so I found my way to the kitchens and garages of the school, and the fact I hung out with *the help* made me a target of a lot of bullying.

"Maria and Paul really did save me. Always welcomed me. Always made a fuss over my strengths. I felt, in all the world, as if they *saw* me. And even better, that they liked what they saw.

"It disappointed my parents immensely when I went into mechanical engineering. It wasn't a prestigious degree. I was supposed to get an MBA, as I was expected to step up and be the CEO of the family businesses.

"They died in a plane crash before I finished college. Maria and Paul were there for me when that happened. Grief is even more complicated when you suddenly realize you are never going to get the moment you waited your whole life for.

"But Maria and Paul gave me what my parents never could. They've been there for me ever since. Both of them should be retired, but they just won't hear of it. I actually bought them a condo in Florida, a few years ago, because Maria's always complaining about how cold winter in New York is."

He chuckled softly, "That lasted about a week. They hated it. They arrived back here with their suitcases. Maria told me she had to have a purpose getting up in the morning. Imagine, me, being someone's reason for getting up in the morning. It's humbling.

"At least she doesn't complain about the weather, anymore."

Sometime, while he told all this, Molly's hand had crept into his, and in that touch, acceptance and encouragement.

Somehow, he had wanted to tell her about his relationship with Maria and Paul, and instead had revealed way too much about himself.

He glanced at Molly. He braced himself for pity in her eyes. Pathetic to have told her this poor little rich boy story, unloved by his parents, bullied at school, turning to the hired help to have his needs met.

But when he looked at Molly, he saw no pity in her steady gaze at all. There was a look of tenderness so deep it could overwhelm a man.

"Now I understand why you're the way you are," she said, softly. "The gift you bring to everyone is that you see their intrinsic value. It's amazing to see someone turn challenges into strengths. It's hopeful. Thank you for telling me."

It occurred to him his lovely assistant was prepared to see him through rose-colored glasses.

And nice as that was, he needed not to read too much into it. In fact, he needed to get things back on track.

The track that he had knocked them off.

He removed his hand from hers. Liam wanted to coax Sunday back; he wanted, suddenly and almost desperately, for things to be the way they had been before.

"So," he said, "what was the most exciting part of tonight, for you?"

She looked taken aback at his sudden shift.

"Can I only pick one?" she asked.

"Okay, two," he conceded.

"Um, you go first."

He had to guide them back to familiar territory. He couldn't risk this relationship—best thing that had ever happened to him, his Woman Sunday—to these kinds of distressing deviations from their norm.

"Okay," he said, pensively. "I thought the widget that controlled air flow to cooling mechanisms on big machines had potential. And of course, Jordan's invention, Fresh, was simply amazing."

For a moment, his unflappable assistant looked completely flummoxed.

"Oh," she said, after a moment, "the most exciting thing from the awards function."

What had she thought he meant?

"Can I see your phone?"

He handed it to her, and she scanned through it. He was close to accomplishing what he wanted, bringing them back to familiar ground, so now was not the time to notice how adorable she looked, the light from his phone reflecting off her glasses and the teeth her tongue was caught between.

"I'm going in a different direction than you," she said. "I liked the all-natural insecticide made out of geraniums. What an incredible way to turn something so abundant into a product *after* its original purpose has been fulfilled."

"I agree, in principle, but it's problematic. How would you possibly collect all the used geraniums? And creating and marketing a one-off product is difficult. She might be better to take that idea to a company that's already producing insecticides or beauty creams."

"Okay, my second favorite was the virtual reality one."

"For swimming pools," he recalled. "That was a good idea. Creating underwater images that could make it seem as if you were swimming with sharks."

"Or on a coral reef. Or in a completely imaginary underwater world."

Just like that, they were themselves again. Even though she was in a housecoat, even though he'd confided something to her that he never told anyone, the awkwardness was gone, and they were fully immersed in the amazing and infinite world of ideas.

When she yawned, he finally realized it was way too late for this.

He got up, and she got up. They stood looking over the New York skyline and then they turned and he found himself looking at her.

"You know," he said, "I think this went amazingly well. What would you think about doing it again? I mean, stepping in as my companion, my plus-one, again sometime? It's so comfortable."

Did she look strangely disappointed by the suggestion?

"Of course," she said. "Whatever works for you, chief."

Somehow his relief at having such a reliable easy-to-be-with companion for events was short-lived.

Because Molly took a deep breath. She stood up on her tiptoes and her lips brushed his cheek.

All that work he'd done to get Sunday back, to get them back on familiar ground, disappeared like mist before a hot sun.

"Thanks for a really fun night. Especially the piggyback ride."

He realized maybe continuing this plus-one charade wasn't going to be quite as comfortable as he thought.

* * *

Molly spun away from Liam, but not before registering the shock in his eyes that she had kissed him.

Good heavens! A benign little *thank-you* for what had been a very fun evening. And an unexpectedly exciting one, too.

Though it showed what different pages they were on, that she thought the most exciting thing about the evening had definitely been the piggyback ride.

Well, until she had kissed him and felt the scrape of his whiskers under her lips.

And meanwhile, Liam thought the most exciting part of the evening was some widget that did something she could barely understand.

She found her way through the apartment back to the beautiful room, and she slipped in and closed the door behind her, leaning into it, thinking of her lips grazing his cheek.

Thinking of him telling her those things about his younger days, entrusting her with confidences that just deepened her sense of falling for him.

So unprofessional! It was an evening of mistakes compounding on each other in that awful way that mistakes tended to do. Forgetting her purse at Second Chances cascading into a series of unpredictable events.

Not one of which she would change.

She noticed a brand-new overnight bag had been set carefully on her bed, and she went over and studied it. It was gorgeous, actually—deep red leather, with beautiful stitching, one of those bags sophisticated people used as carry-ons.

She opened it.

It felt like Christmas morning. Brand-new pajamas. A pair of plain black yoga pants and a white V-necked T-shirt for tomorrow. Socks. Comfy loafers. Some plain underwear, cotton panties, a pull-on, one-size-fits-all sports bra. A toothbrush and toothpaste. She'd even been provided with a rudimentary makeup bag filled with little pots of eyeshadow, a mascara tube, lip gloss, a compact with blush in it. Surprisingly, there was a mini–first aid kit, and when she peeked inside it, everything that was needed for blister-aid was there.

And if she hadn't told Liam she didn't like her feet being touched, would he have looked after the foot first aid? The very thought made her shiver. She made herself focus on the delights she had found in the bag.

It looked as if Maria had guessed her sizes perfectly.

Molly put on her new pajamas, and climbed between the crisp linen sheets. She had read, of course, about thread counts and Egyptian cotton.

Until you experienced it, it was way too easy to dismiss such luxuries as all hype, as just people with too much money finding new and exotic ways to spend it.

But nestled into those sheets, the bed deeply comfortable, the apartment silent around her, she wondered if she had ever felt quite so safe.

She fell asleep instantly.

When she woke, though, to the morning light filtering through the bedroom window, the feeling of safety was gone. Molly contemplated the awkward intimacy of being in her boss's house, her lips still feeling oddly *changed* for having scraped across his cheek.

Her predicament was really not much different from last night. She still didn't have her purse, so she was going to have to find something to do with herself until Second Chances opened. She didn't even have her phone to find out what time that was!

Well, one thing—he wasn't seeing her in her pajamas.

Except he'd already seen her in a housecoat, so that barn door had already been left open. Still, it wasn't too late to start doing some damage control. Walls had come down last night. For both of them.

It was tempting to want them to stay down, but no, that was completely unacceptable.

He wasn't dealing with her dirty laundry, either. She stuffed the pajamas from last night in the bag. She went and gathered the dress off the bathroom floor. It was a mess, worse because she had left it in a heap. She wasn't sure it could be saved, but maybe it could, with careful hand laundering. And she *was* one of the few people left on the planet who had an iron and knew how to use it. The dress joined her new pajamas in the overnight bag.

She showered, put on her new clothes, scraped her hair back extra severely. She looked in the full-length mirror and it made her happy that she could pass for any other woman in NYC on a Saturday morning. She dressed her blisters and gave into the temptation of a slight dusting of makeup.

She opened her door to find a bag on the handle. She peered in it.

All her things she had left at Second Chances were there, her purse on top. She went back into the room, closed the door and sank on the bed.

This was what *she* did. She solved problems. She put out fires. She looked after others. It was astonishing to find herself in the position of the one being looked after.

Actually, it made her want to weep.

Since she felt like weeping, anyway, she pulled her phone out of the bag and braced herself for messages—probably increasingly hysterical when Molly couldn't be reached—from her mother.

The phone was one hundred percent completely dead.

Finally, she gathered herself and left her room. She heard a clatter of dishes and followed the sound to the kitchen.

Maria was busy. She turned and smiled at Molly. "You're up. Did you sleep well? What can I make you for breakfast?"

She seemed, embarrassingly, to know what was on top of Molly's mind.

Where was Liam?

"Liam's left for the gym already," Maria said.

Of course. Molly knew that. It was right there

on the schedule she looked at every day. Saturday at 6 a.m. he went to the gym. Why had she thought today was going to be different?

Did she seriously think he would feel as eager to see her again as she had been to see him?

"Waffles? French toast?"

There was no excuse to stay here! Molly had her keys. She had her wallet. She could stop and pick up a bagel anywhere along the way home.

But it was hard to give up this feeling of someone looking after her for a change.

"Waffles would be lovely."

Maria busied herself mixing batter and heating what looked to be an ancient waffle maker.

"Thank you for finding all those things for me," Molly said, as she dug into the delectable homemade treat a little later. "It couldn't have been easy in the middle of the night. And having my stuff returned before the store even opened."

"Things?" Maria said, genuinely puzzled. "What things? What store?"

CHAPTER TEN

"YOU KNOW. The items I found in my room last night. Pajamas." Molly gestured down at herself. "What I'm wearing. And my stuff that I forgot at Second Chances."

"I'm sorry, I don't know what you're talking about."

Startled, Molly realized that Maria hadn't provided her with these emergency items. Which meant her boss had. Liam must have been arranging a delivery while she'd been in the shower last night.

And he must have been up at the crack of dawn pulling strings to get her stuff out of the closed store.

Maybe Liam didn't need her nearly as much as he said he did.

It seemed he was quite capable of being a Man Friday, all by himself.

An hour later, she said goodbye to Maria and did a final check of her room: towels neatly folded over the shower bar, tub and sink left spotless, bed made.

With a sigh, Molly realized it wasn't just hard to give up being looked after, but hard to say goodbye, period. It wasn't just the luxury, it was the *feeling* she had here of deep serenity, of a world that unfolded in an orderly manner all the time.

It was the sense of being safe somehow, deeper than anything she had ever felt before.

Still, she made herself shut the door firmly on the bedroom she'd been provided, and she went to the front mezzanine where they had come in last night.

Her hand on the elevator button, she took one more look around, as if she could memorize the beauty of this space and tuck it away inside her for those times when chaos came.

And with a family like hers, those times were inevitable.

Her eyes caught on the wastebasket, tucked under the entry table. The shoes from last night were still in it.

The reason for the piggyback ride. Her very own glass slippers, really, that had carried her into her unexpected night in this Cinderella world. Whether it was the poor girl in her, or whether she planned to have them bronzed, she wasn't sure. But she could not bear the thought of those shoes being tossed away.

She fished them from the wastebasket and zipped them inside her new bag.

The subway brought her crashing back to the reality of life. Even though it was Saturday, it was crowded. She couldn't find a place to sit. She stepped in gum. The man beside her smelled bad. Another snored loudly from his seat.

Just yesterday, she had *loved* the subway, the quintessential New York experience.

Unfortunately, her brush with lifestyles of the rich and famous also tainted how she felt about her space.

She stepped in the door of her tiny, beloved basement suite and waited for *that* feeling. Being home.

Just yesterday she had *loved* this space.

Now all of it—her secondhand finds, the tightness of the space, poor Winspear sitting in the light of the one tiny window—seemed faintly tawdry.

And that was *exactly* the problem with experimenting with a station above your own in life. It was exactly as her mother had warned her—about getting *ideas*.

It planted the seeds of dissatisfaction. It made a person greedily want *more*. Molly thought of how hard it had felt to leave the quiet sanctuary of Liam's apartment this morning.

She had an awful flash memory of her father drinking, before he'd disappeared from their lives forever.

Drink after drink after drink.

There was *never* enough to soothe his sense of not having or being enough.

She drew in a deep breath, ordered herself to stop it, immediately. There were things to do. The dress to save, shoes to clean. Winspear to look after.

Chocolates to arrange for Liam's trip.

She fell on the last task with the enthusiasm and focus of an underfed dog who had been thrown a bone.

After a while, she remembered to plug in her phone. As she had guessed, there were many messages from her mother and several missed calls.

She listened, with a sinking heart, to the messages. The lawyer needed a ten-thousand-dollar retainer.

People, Molly realized, thought ten thousand dollars was a lot of money, until they had a legal problem.

Her phone rang. It was her mother, and she didn't want to talk to her, didn't want all that shrill desperation to take the shine of her evening with Liam away from her.

Stressed, she checked her bank account. Not enough, but it would have to do. She sent it.

She got a text from her mother within seconds.

Not an ounce of gratitude.

When can you come up with the rest?

Molly deliberately turned her phone back off. She'd never been so happy to see the inside of her office as she was on Monday.

It had become her sanctuary. She could not risk everything this place gave her because she was having extremely complicated feelings about her boss.

Whom, despite knowing better, she couldn't wait to see.

And he did not disappoint. As soon as Liam came in the door, she felt something in her go calm, as if everything in her world was going to be alright.

If Liam felt any awkwardness at Molly's unexpected stay at his apartment, it didn't show at all.

She pulled the red leather bag out from under her desk. "I'll return this to you."

He squinted at it, then waved his hand. "Oh, no need."

He asked after her feet. If the memory of piggybacking her blazed through his mind the way it did hers, it didn't show.

After assuring him her feet were fine, she moved on quickly, wanting to get his focus away from her because it was just too easy to bask in his caring.

Briskly, all business, Molly briefed him about the week.

"You leave for Québec City early Wednesday evening to sign the final agreement with Maple You Do, Maple You Don't on Thursday. It'll be a day of meetings, leaving early Thursday evening. I've sent your itinerary to your phone but here's a printed copy for you. And here's the booklet."

She'd gotten in the habit of preparing a briefing book for him when he went on any trip, even a short one. This time she'd included notes about the maple syrup industry, a bit of the history of Québec and Québec City, and a bit of background on the small family business that had grown too fast and needed exactly the kind of help FIX provided.

She'd left out anything about Québec's amazing

chocolate industry. That would be her surprise to him when he got there.

He thumbed through the book, pleased, and then looked up at her. "It's definitely a poster child case of what I always wanted FIX to be, a company that helps other companies be the most they can be with just a few simple changes to their operating efficiencies and marketing.

"You've put a lot into this booklet, for a visit that really amounts to less than twenty-four hours."

She could feel the heat rush to her cheeks. "I'm sorry," she stammered. "You're right. I spent much too much time on it."

It occurred to her she was getting way too used to running the show.

Too big for her britches, her mother would say.

"Have you been to Québec City before?" she asked.

"Yes."

"I'm mortified," she said. "I should have really checked that before I spent so much time on preparing—"

"Sunday, stop. I don't feel like you wasted your time. Or mine. These advance preps you do for me are invaluable. Don't change a thing."

But she knew she would. Already she was noting, *less time researching short trip destinations. Check if he's been there before.*

"You loved putting this briefing together, didn't you?"

Oh! The last thing she wanted was for her *loves* to be so transparent.

"I did," she admitted. She shouldn't elaborate, but she did. "I read a book about a little girl, set in Québec City in the 1700s. It's been on my bucket list since then."

He cocked his head at her. "Really?"

"Really."

"Well, that's an easy one to fulfill. Is your passport in order?"

"Yes, it is." She'd applied for a passport when she was sixteen years old. Silly, really, a girl from a backwater with no hope of ever going anywhere. But having that document had felt as if she had a secret key that could open whole worlds to her.

And now look! Still…

"Oh," she said, embarrassed. "I wasn't hinting."

Had she sounded as wistful as she felt? She was really becoming much too transparent to her boss.

"Of course you weren't hinting! But the more I think about it, the more I like the idea. Sunday, clear your schedule. It'll be a kind of combination assistant and my plus-one. I mean, one day isn't much, but we'll manage to squeeze in a traipse through the Old City. Bring good walking shoes. See? You'll need that bag again, after all."

Of course, that was truer than he knew because she certainly didn't have any appropriate luggage for a business trip.

On a private plane, a voice inside her squealed.

It caused a disturbing sense of weakness in

Molly that her boss could make dreams come true so casually, in the absolute blink of an eye.

In her world, dreams were something you hankered after, *forever*, bracing yourself inwardly for the unlikely possibility of them ever materializing.

What was she going to do now? Say no?

"It's only for one day, Molly. You'll be home safe in your own bed by Thursday night."

He hardly ever called her Molly, and especially not with that aching note of gentleness in his voice, as if it was evident to him that she was such a creature of habit that this change in plan was throwing her for a loop.

It wasn't really a weakness to give in, Molly told herself. Liam was her boss, after all. He was telling her how it was going to be. She couldn't really argue with him.

"I'll book an extra room," she said, keeping her tone as professional as possible, when inside her doubts gave way to something completely different.

In fact, a little renegade voice was singing—*singing*—in her. *Québec City. And Liam.*

Of course, she had known eventually there would be a trip she accompanied him on. Maxine had travelled with Liam several times a year.

Somehow Molly had expected she would be *ready* for it. That she would have weeks or even months to prepare and plan.

On Tuesday night, she could barely sleep she was so nervous and excited. She got up three times to check that she had put her passport in her purse. Then she lay awake going over every possibility. She'd only been on a plane once before, on that trip to Los Angeles. It had made her feel queasy. What if she got sick, this time? Plus, this time there was an extra challenge. She'd never crossed an international border before, but she'd watched reality television shows about it.

What if her brother's latest brush with the law put a red flag beside her name? Or her father's ancient history came back to haunt her? What if she was questioned in front of Liam?

What if they said she couldn't enter Canada?

That little doubt that was never far away—*you aren't good enough, you're an imposter*—flared to life.

She got up and looked at the outfit she had laid out. It had to be appropriate for a day at the office and the later afternoon trip.

She had chosen a dark jacket and skirt, a plain blouse and flat shoes that would be good for walking if they did have a short opportunity to see Old Québec. She only kept the blouse and shoes as she laid out a new outfit.

She traded out the skirt for pencil line black slacks and the jacket for a gray hand-knit sweater. Very grandmotherly, a more trustworthy look for the customs officials. Then she traded out the blouse for a patterned one that might hide stains better if she spilled coffee during turbulence or worse, got sick on herself.

She double-checked what she had packed for Thursday, another plain skirt and solid-colored blouse. The flat shoes should be good for both days, and comfortable for walking.

It was a nerve-wracking day at the office, partly due to her lack of sleep. She was glad Liam was off-site today, because she'd had enough trouble concentrating. For some reason, every little noise, even the phone ringing, made her jump, and she wouldn't have wanted him to see that.

She hadn't been able to eat because her stomach was so butterfly-ey. Molly finally stepped onto the FIX private jet early Wednesday evening. She had outwardly—she hoped—tamed her anxiety, but inwardly she was a mess.

Coming off the loading bridge, she paused at the entry door to the cabin. She could barely hear the crew member's warm welcome over the buzz in her ears.

Molly was suddenly aware there were some things you could never prepare for. Being on a private jet was one of them.

She definitely did not belong here. But still, she took it all in, like an awed visitor being given a glimpse of the crown jewels.

Like the interior of Liam's apartment, the interior of the jet oozed an atmosphere of calm, luxury and wealth.

Stepping into the cabin was like stepping into

a very posh living room. A deep, creamy leather couch faced a highly polished cabinet with exquisite wood grains. A bar, she deduced.

Farther along, four leather reclining-style seats faced each other, forming a conversation group. Behind that was a dining table, and then a door, slightly open to reveal a sumptuous bedroom.

Liam arrived, coming in the door behind her. He practically bumped into her, as she was glued to the spot.

"Hey, Sunday. You made it," he said. "Pick a place to sit. The recliners are the most comfortable if you're going to read. This sofa is the best for watching a movie or television. A screen pops out of that console."

She contemplated the fact that people watched television while travelling hundreds of miles an hour at thirty thousand feet. She had not even looked at the screen on the back of her seat on that first flight to Los Angeles.

This seemed even more surreal, almost too much to handle.

She turned and stared at him, paralyzed, hoping she would find something in his familiar face that would calm the anxiety inside her.

"Sunday! I didn't picture you as a nervous flyer, somehow."

Oh! Again, she did not like the fact that Liam seemed to be getting better and better at reading her. And if it was only flying! It was all of it. Crossing a border. Being out of her depth. This was not the office, which had become such a comfort zone.

This was a brand-new world, and a brand-new way of being with Liam, and Molly felt hopelessly out of her depth.

CHAPTER ELEVEN

MOLLY'S SENSE OF being an absolute bundle of nerves was not diminished by Liam's presence. In fact, she felt it would make her seem incredibly unworldly if she admitted to her boss she was quite the newbie to air travel.

Before that trip to LA, the longest trip of her life had been by bus from Louisiana to New York, her newly acquired diploma from Mrs. Michael's School of Business laid carefully, so as not to get folded, in the bottom of her worn suitcase.

She'd found out, and quickly too, when she'd started applying for jobs, that her diploma was laughable.

Where she came from, Mrs. Michael's was considered an institute of higher education, not to mention an affordable one.

Attending Mrs. Michael's was bound to give her highfalutin ideas about herself, according to her mother.

Molly had been lucky to get on at the mail room at FIX. It was really nothing less than a miracle.

And she would have to say the very same thing

about her, Molly Littleton, being on board a private jet in any capacity.

She wondered what her mother would think about this.

She'd want more money—that's what she'd think about it.

Molly made her way, unsteadily, as if they were already in the air, to the group of recliners, sat down, squeezed the armrests.

"I knew you'd pick reading," Liam said, taking the seat beside her. "Do up your seat belt. Don't recline until after we've taken off."

"Aye, aye, chief," she said, and her nerves calmed ever so slightly, though she knew relaxing totally was out of the question. And she was right. From the thrust of takeoff, to all the strange sounds and the little bumps, it felt to Molly, this time, as it had last, as if flying was completely unnatural.

Liam's parents had *died* in a plane crash.

How could he be sitting there, calmly opening his briefcase and accepting a coffee from the flight crew?

She herself did not accept coffee. Or snacks. Despite choosing an outfit that took in the possibility of accidents, Molly had a sense of needing to maintain control over every element that she possibly could. No splashing coffee cups for her! No admittedly delicious smelling meal to add to her stomach turmoil.

She actually felt worse when they finally landed

than she had when they'd taken off. To her, this was the most terrifying part of the trip.

She felt like a spy she had once read about crossing Checkpoint Charlie from East Berlin to West Berlin right after the Second World War, the lives of dozens of people riding on his successful crossing.

"Where do we clear customs?" she asked Liam. Her voice sounded tiny.

"Oh, they'll come to us." He didn't even look up from what he was doing.

Sure enough, when the sealed door was opened, the cabin crew welcomed officials from Canada Customs on board.

The man and woman chatted with the crew for a moment, then made their way back toward Liam and Molly.

Nothing good in her entire life had ever come from people wearing uniforms! She had been raised with a good healthy suspicion of all authority figures.

She felt as if her heart was going to beat out of her chest as she passed her passport, slightly damp from her sweating palms, to the border official.

"Is everything all right, miss?" one of the officials asked.

Checkpoint Charlie. Checkpoint Charlie. Breathe. Smile.

"Yes," she said, "everything's fine."

"I think she's scared of flying," Liam said, passing them his own passport.

"Ah, well, you're safely on the ground now. *Bienvenue au Canada.* Welcome to Canada. Enjoy your stay."

"That's it?" she whispered to Liam, when they turned and left. After all her inward rehearsing of answering questions calmly and articulately, she wasn't sure which feeling was more acute: Relief. Or disappointment.

He gave her a look. "What were you expecting?"

She lifted a shoulder. "A few questions, maybe. Some *interest*."

"Huh, you don't look like the type they are interested in."

Was he saying she didn't look interesting?

"What are you hiding from me, Sunday?"

It felt as if her heart stopped beating in her chest.

"What?" she whispered.

He squinted at her appraisingly. "Ah," he said. "International jewel thief."

And then he grinned. She realized he wasn't sniffing out some truth about her family; he was *teasing* her.

"America's Most Wanted, Top Ten," he guessed again and then sighed dramatically. "It's always the ones you least suspect."

A long way off, and too close at the same time.

"I just thought at the very least, I'd get my passport stamped," she said, trying to keep it as light as he was keeping it.

"If we ask them, they will," he said, with an indulgent smile.

"No," she said hastily, "it's fine." She was not inviting more scrutiny from Canada Border Services! With her passport back in her hand, she considered the fact it was official: She, Molly Littleton, had been admitted into a foreign country. Welcomed, in two languages!

Liam was looking at her closely. "You've never crossed a border before, have you?"

"Only my second time on a plane," she admitted. What had happened to not telling him that? As if he couldn't tell!

"Wow," he said. "Almost a vir—"

He stopped abruptly. "You did great, Sunday."

He had, very wisely, decided against a comment on virginity. Instead, he had paid her a small compliment. Small as it was, it felt like wind lifting sagging sails. For the first time she allowed excitement to outweigh the anxiety.

For the most part, every single adventure she had ever been on was inside the covers of a book. If you didn't count her family shenanigans, which were never the kind of adventures anyone in their right mind would sign up for.

Real adventures were more nerve-racking than she'd expected. But if she had to venture outside her comfort zone, could she have been assigned a better guide than Liam?

Liam watched Molly as the limousine whisked them away from the airport and into Québec City.

She'd flown twice.

She'd never been in another country.

Now, she was craning her neck. Even though evening darkness had fallen, she was trying to see everything.

"Look," she breathed, "there's one of the gates into Old Québec. Did you know it's the only fortified city north of Mexico?"

"I didn't," he said.

"This is one of the oldest European settlements in North America," his living, breathing encyclopedia told him. "Old Québec is a UNESCO World Heritage site."

When they got out of the car at the hotel, she turned and stared across the street.

"I can't believe we're staying right here," she said. "This is what I wanted to see the most. The Parliament Building of Québec."

Not the shopping, he thought wryly, not the world-class restaurants. No, the parliament buildings.

He followed her gaze. The structure did look magnificent, especially lit up at night.

"It was inspired by the Louvre Palace in Paris," she said, with a sigh. "There's a tour, if our schedule permits. After our meetings tomorrow. I mean, I'd go on my own time, of course."

He could tell her to go while he was in meetings tomorrow, but he couldn't bring himself to do it.

"No, I'd like to see it, too."

Which surprised the hell out of him, because he'd been to Québec City many times and it had never once occurred to him that he would like to take a tour of the Parliament Building.

He realized, suddenly, it had nothing to do with the Louvre-inspired buildings, as magnificent as they were.

It was about *her*, somehow.

It was about Molly.

Liam had travelled the entire world. He moved in circles where people had everything. They had private planes and helicopters and estates. Sometimes they owned multiple estates and homes situated everywhere on the globe. They had stables full of horses and garages full of cars.

And they had done everything. They had experienced the most iconic beaches in the world, been to the rainforests, gone on safari in Africa, helicopter-skied in the Rockies. They had dined at every five-star restaurant in every major city on all five continents and shopped at the most exclusive stores on the planet.

He knew those people. That was his world. That was the world he'd grown up with and the world he still lived in.

Nothing thrilled. Nothing excited. The people in the small circles of the extraordinarily wealthy weren't exactly jaundiced by new experiences, but bored? Maybe.

Even as a kid, he'd been different. He'd found things interesting that other people overlooked. How things worked fascinated him. He'd come to find his satisfaction in the endless frontier of new ideas rather than in collecting things, in testing the limits of experiences.

As for the parliament buildings, he was not going to miss Molly experiencing the world with such freshness and such wonder.

She was, he realized, looking extra plain today. She wore no makeup at all, and her hair was pulled back sternly. She was wearing a gray sweater that looked like something someone would wear who owned a cat and crocheted doilies in their spare time.

The outfit, thankfully, hid all those luscious curves he had seen the night they'd gotten wet together.

And yet, despite that, despite what he suspected was a deliberately toned-down appearance, she was radiating a soft beauty.

He could feel her energy reaching across the chilly night and filling him with an odd warmth.

Looking at her face as she gazed toward those parliament buildings, it occurred to him that she looked as alive, somehow, as he had ever seen her.

If he saw Québec City through her eyes, whatever that was shining so softly from her was going to be contagious. He was going to feel brand-new in some way he had not felt before.

And he just wasn't sure if that was a threat.

Or a promise.

It was only for one day, he told himself.

"Are you hungry?" he asked her, realizing suddenly she had eaten nothing on the plane.

"Absolutely starving."

"Have you ever had poutine?"

"What?"

"Ah, *finally* something you have never heard of."

"What is it?"

"A Québec staple. French fries, drenched in gravy and cheese curds."

"Well, that sounds perfectly horrible."

"Doesn't it?" he said, pleasantly. "It's caught on in other places, now. You can even get it in New York. But it's never the same as having it here. My favorite is duck-duck. The french fries cooked in duck tallow and the poutine topped with duck meat."

"It's sounding worse and worse," she said, with the cutest little wrinkle of her nose.

Liam, he warned himself, *do not start seeing Sunday as cute.*

But it was too late for that. After getting caught in the rain with her last week, he was never going to see her the same way again, anyway.

"I've never had duck," she said, pensively.

That word *virgin* popped into his head again.

"Well, let's make it a complete day of firsts, shall we?"

She looked doubtful.

"Duck is very prevalent in Québec culture and cuisine," he told her.

She still looked unconvinced.

"Sunday! Trust me."

A man could live for the look that lit up her eyes in that moment.

CHAPTER TWELVE

"Of course I trust you!" Molly said to Liam.

He glanced at his watch. Québec was in the same time zone as New York. There should be plenty of places to eat that were still open. And so they checked in and dropped off their bags.

The concierge recommended a restaurant just blocks away, in the Old City, renowned for its duck-duck.

And so, walking past the lit parliament buildings and under an archway in the thick stone wall that surrounded Old Québec, Liam was aware of beginning an amazing journey of witnessing Molly as she discovered brand-new things.

She did not disappoint!

Of course, Old Québec was an absolute enchantment, certainly one of the most beautiful cities Liam had ever been in, but its beauty deepened around him as Molly noticed everything with complete wonder. Cobblestones, dates on buildings, the flowers in window boxes.

He held open the door for her of the restaurant that had been recommended.

"*Bonjour. Bienvenue.*" They were greeted by a lone waiter who seemed to also be acting as the maître d'.

"*Bonjour,*" Molly offered haltingly, and then she won over the waiter completely by adding, just as haltingly, "*Comment allez-vous?*"

He beamed at her, then switched seamlessly to English.

"I am wonderful," he said. "Is there any other way to be on a beautiful spring evening in Québec City?"

No, Liam realized, as they were shown their table, there was absolutely no other way to be.

"Especially," the waiter said, pulling out chairs for them with flourish, "if you are lovers."

Molly's eyes went very wide and her mouth opened and then snapped shut, as she looked at Liam helplessly to correct the misinterpretation.

"Just business associates," Liam said to the waiter, who looked pleased, as if he might have been fishing for this very information.

After the waiter left, Molly deliberately looked at everything but Liam.

Again, no detail went unnoticed: the ancient hardwood floors, the blackened timbers of the roof, the depth of the sill of the window they were seated at.

"Oh, my gosh," she said, touching the stone, "the wall must be three feet thick."

The waiter doted on them—Liam was pretty sure he was flirting shamelessly. Liam noticed, faintly amused but mostly annoyed, that despite her downplayed appearance the man was like a moth, drawn to her light.

And indeed, Molly was radiating happiness.

Liam wondered, *did that mean she'd been unhappy before?*

Liam realized this was the second time he'd been with her that she had attracted male attention. He'd practically had to chase that guy off her at the awards dinner, too.

It occurred to him that these young men were seeing something about Molly that he'd missed.

He found himself studying her.

It hit him like a bolt of lightning. Yes, there it was.

It wasn't just her wonder, or her curiosity.

It was passion.

Burning right below the surface of her reliable Sunday self.

"What?" she asked him, self-consciously taking a sip of her water.

With relief, he realized it wasn't passion, after all.

"You still have the eyelashes on," he said.

That was it! Men were suckers for things like that.

"Oh," she said, glumly. "I think they attached these things with construction glue."

She seemed totally unaware she was being flirted with by the waiter. Liam consulted with her over the menu.

"Poutine, for sure."

"Don't order two," she said and did that wrinkled nose thing. He hoped the waiter didn't see it, because it was as compelling, somehow, as her eyelashes.

"Could I just try yours? I don't think I'm going to like it. I'll have the meat pie."

He contemplated that. Being with a woman who was conscious about wasting things, who didn't order one of each item on the menu and take a single bite simply because he could afford it.

That's what Charlotte had been like. It was good to remember her, the woman who had so charmed him that he had nearly married her.

It was good to remember Charlotte as Molly was suggesting eating off his plate, which seemed extraordinarily intimate.

"Get your own," he said. "You're going to like it."

When the waiter came back he ordered.

"Two poutine," the waiter repeated, with approval. He pronounced it poo-tin.

"It makes me nervous. I haven't had it before," she confided.

"What? A virgin!"

He effortlessly used the word Liam had avoided earlier.

"You will not be disappointed," he promised Molly with a fiendish wag of his eyebrows.

"I don't know. I'm being talked into it against my better judgment."

"Ah," the waiter said smoothly, "sometimes overcoming judgment is the best way in life, yes?"

"Oh," she said, very vehemently. "No!"

She *still* didn't know the waiter was flirting. Liam caught his eye and raised a warning brow.

The man lifted a shoulder, as if to say *but you said you're just business associates.*

And that was true. Were these feelings of protectiveness within the realm of that relationship?

Thankfully, Molly didn't notice the wordless interchange between Liam and her new admirer.

She had her phone out. "The last tour of the Parliament Building is at 4:30 tomorrow afternoon. What do you think? Will we be done meetings by then? Can we squeeze it in? Should I book?"

He suddenly didn't want her to *squeeze* anything in. He wanted to keep that look on her face forever.

She was the best assistant he had ever had. Why not show his appreciation of her? Good Lord, the waiter was doing a better job of appreciating her than he was.

He'd surprise her with an extra day in Québec City. They could go sightseeing together on Friday.

"I'll look after it," he said.

She put away her phone and gazed up at the ceiling. "Can't you just feel it? All the years? All the people? Life unfolding over the centuries. Love and sorrow?"

The thing was he *could feel* it.

There was that passion again. He was kidding

himself that it was the eyelashes. Though they did do incredible things to her eyes.

The poutine arrived. She stared at it, her expression horrified. Liam saw it through her eyes.

Okay, definitely not the most visually attractive dish in the world. In fact, it looked like something that hadn't agreed with the cat.

But she was aware of the waiter hovering and of course, so was he. The look he gave him did not move him along.

Both men watched as she picked up her fork.

She toyed with the topping and then took a deep breath. She speared a french fry covered in goopy gravy and white chunks of curd. Dark duck meat clung to the top of it. She regarded her fork with dismay, then closed her eyes and popped the morsel in her mouth.

The startling combination of flavors registered. The look on her face, Liam thought, should really be reserved for private moments. Very private moments.

Her eyes flew open.

"*Mon Dieu,*" she exclaimed.

The waiter chortled with delight, while Liam looked at the tiny little gravy spot that graced her bottom lip. Her tongue darted out and flicked it.

Mon dieu, indeed, he thought.

"I'll have whatever she's having," the waiter said, paraphrasing a very famous line from a movie. He moved away, pleased, as if that line was invented by him, and he had cooked the dish himself.

Molly looked after him, a tiny frown playing across her lips, her brows dropped.

"Was he…" she whispered, searching for words and turning back to Liam, wide-eyed.

"Coming on to you?" Liam asked dryly.

She looked every bit as horrified as she had when the dish had first been set in front of her.

But then she giggled.

And he found the humor in it, too.

And then they were both laughing, and he realized she was not the only one drenched in happiness.

"I loved that," Molly said, the following afternoon, after the tour of the parliament buildings was done. They were standing on the front steps. Their hotel was a two-minute walk away. They would go get their things and then it would be over.

She looked out over Québec City. *Au revoir*, she thought, but she didn't say it out loud. She knew all her longing would be in that phrase, naked for Liam to see.

Coming here, this spontaneous trip, had been such a gift. The dinner last night. The meetings today. It had been amazing to see Liam at work outside the office. He had never once made her feel like just an assistant or even introduced her that way.

He had coaxed her opinions out of her, made her feel like a contributing member of the team.

To see him in action had made it clear why he had enjoyed such success at what he did.

"I guess we should go get our things and head for the airport," she said. "I scheduled the flight for seven. If we call for a car—"

"I cancelled the flight."

"What?"

"And extended our rooms for one more night."

"What?" she asked again, her voice a whisper this time. Her longing had been naked after all. But what was astonishing was that it had influenced him.

"I rescheduled the flight for the same time tomorrow and kept the hotel rooms," he said.

"You knew about this this morning," she said. "That's why you told me to leave my bag in my room."

He laughed. "You absolutely hate spontaneity, don't you?"

Well, yes, she did, but she could also feel everything she believed starting to shift uncomfortably within her. Like, for instance, her belief—*good things don't happen to people like me*.

"I can't just whisk you away when you've hardly seen any of it. It's on your bucket list, after all."

Molly had to turn rapidly away from her boss. She was going to cry. He had extended the stay for her and for her only.

She had never had anyone do anything quite so special for her before.

"If we're staying an extra day, I'll have to rearrange

your appointments for tomorrow," she said, after she had gathered herself.

"No worries. I already looked after it."

"Do you need me at all?" she asked.

"Of course I do, Sunday. That's what this is all about. To let you know how much I need you. And appreciate you."

She still had her face tilted away from him, but he crooked his finger under her chin and turned it to him.

"Are you crying?"

"Of course I'm not crying!" she said, lifting her glasses and taking a swipe at her eyes.

He frowned, pressed a gentle finger against the corner of her eye, regarded it thoughtfully. "Wet," he deduced.

"Well, maybe a little. I'm easily overwhelmed."

"That's a side of you that doesn't show at work."

"Because that's a controlled environment."

"This is why you don't like surprises," he said.

She wanted to tell him she had very little experience with *nice* surprises. On the other hand, she did not want him probing that dark corner of her life, a place that—if she could not leave it entirely behind her—at least she did not have to show to others.

CHAPTER THIRTEEN

THANKFULLY, AFTER gazing at her quizzically for a moment, Liam took Molly's cue to move on.

"Do you have enough clothes?" he asked her. "For an extra day?"

"Oh." This was what spontaneity did. A cascading effect of more and more problems to be solved as a result.

"I can make do."

"I can't," he said. "Let's go get a few things and then go for dinner."

Everything in his world was so fluid and uncomplicated. Money might not be able to buy happiness, but it seemed to be able to buy just about everything else. It would be too easy to get used to this, to want it.

She had to keep her defenses up. She just had to!

But when they stopped at the first little boutique they came across just inside the walls of the Old City, she realized her defenses had been crumbling for a long time. And shopping together—again—was just the nudge needed for them to be completely destroyed.

"Do you know we were doing exactly this a week ago?" she said. "Shopping?"

He grinned at her. "How about that? It's our plus-one-iversary."

She found herself smiling back at him.

"And this—" Liam held up a red plaid lumberjack-style shirt "—would be the perfect way to celebrate. This would look good on you."

He was teasing her, again. It would all just be so easy to get used to—the light banter, shopping together, a life of *nice* surprises.

She knew it couldn't last. She knew she shouldn't be *playing* with something that meant so much to her—her job, her relationship with her boss. Loving him from afar had felt quite safe before and ever so predictable. These rapid developments since last Friday should be regarded with her customary caution toward change.

On the other hand, the changes were already in motion. She was aware she was as helpless to stop them as she would be standing in front of a moving train with her hand up.

For once in her life, could she stop ferreting out the potential for disaster? Could she stop anticipating impending doom? Could she just go with it? Relax and enjoy?

Tentatively, Molly plucked a shirt off the rack. "Oh, look, there's a matching one for you."

"Let's try them," he suggested, and in unison they pulled the beautifully made woolen shirts over their business clothes.

He regarded her thoughtfully, laughter making the colors spark in his eyes like gold dust catching the light.

"Not quite there," he decided, and he looked around the store. "Aha!"

He snatched a fur-lined aviator-style hat from a loaded shelf. He plopped it on her head, and tied the string tightly under her chin.

Then, he turned and got a similar fur-lined cap for himself, and did the same thing.

He looked outrageous, adorable and completely unselfconscious in his hokey tourist version of a *Québecois*.

He took out his phone, and they hammed it up for selfies.

"Those photos are top secret," she told him, after he put the phone away. "I don't want anyone in the office to see that."

"To see Miss Littleton having fun?" he chided her mildly.

"Exactly!" But then she couldn't help but add, "Do you think people at the office perceive me as uptight?"

Unspoken: *Do you?*

"I don't think I've ever heard anybody say anything that wasn't pure admiration of your organizational skills and memory. Though, once, Smith, in accounting, said you reminded him of his small-town librarian."

"And a higher compliment could not be paid!

That's what I always wanted to be when I was growing up."

"Really? Why?"

"From the first moment I stepped in a library, I was in love. Even before I understood about the worlds hidden within the covers of books, I found the order was so appealing, the calm, the quiet."

"So what got in the way?"

She already felt she'd said way too much. Wasn't the natural question that might be asked *why* did she need order so badly? Calm? Quiet?

She was not sharing the hard fact that life got in the way of her dream. A degree in library arts was as far away for her as a trip to the moon. Mrs. Michael's School of Business had been a bad enough budget stretcher, never mind a real live university.

But she wasn't sharing any of that with Liam.

"It's a dangerous field," she said, and then she leaned in and whispered to him, "Men have fantasies about librarians."

It was uncharacteristically bold, but who wanted to be seen as uptight all the time? Besides, there was something about wearing a fur-lined aviator cap that gave her the courage to step out of her self-imposed mold.

Liam reared back from her, stunned. And then he shouted with laughter.

"They do, indeed," he said. "Just ask the waiter from last night."

"Why would he have thought I was a librarian?"

"Not a librarian, precisely. The *type*."

"What type is that?"

"You know. Glasses. Hand-knit sweater, don't-mess-with-me bun."

Since that was *exactly* the fade-into-the-background look she'd been trying for, why was she slightly offended?

"But I think people suspect there is a layer to you that you keep hidden. And it intrigues."

That was somehow both reassuring that she wasn't a complete frump, and at the very same time, hit too close to home.

She took off the shirt and the hat. "I suppose we'd better find something more suitable," she said.

A half hour later, purchases wrapped in brown paper, Liam insisting on carrying them, they made their way back to the hotel.

"I'll knock on your door in, what, half an hour? Is that enough time?"

When the knock came to her door, she opened it and Liam was standing there looking not like himself at all in jeans and a button-down shirt rolled up at the sleeves. His hair was still wet from the shower.

She was wearing the casual slacks and blouse she had bought. Against her better judgment, she had let her hair down, and she was glad she had because of the way his gaze lingered there for a moment.

The only other time she'd seen Liam casual was a week ago, in his pajamas.

It occurred to her that his charisma, that aura of

confidence he carried himself with, had nothing to do with thousand-dollar suits.

It still oozed off him even when he wore very casual jeans.

And he was eating chocolate. Eating chocolate was a very sexy look on him.

"Did you get some of this?" he asked.

"No."

"You have to try it. I wonder why you didn't get any? There was a basket of it in my room."

See? She did have secrets, and maybe more of them than she wanted.

But this one delighted her. That she gave him secret gifts and he had no idea they were from her.

"Let's go get some dinner," he said.

"You're ruining yours with chocolate."

"There's something you need to know about life. Chocolate does not ever ruin anything."

He broke her off a piece and handed it to her. She popped it in her mouth. It was exquisite. It felt oddly and wonderfully sensual to be sharing chocolate she had secretly given him, as if it was infused with a magic potion.

That promised the most illusive thing of all. The thing money could not buy.

Happiness.

Molly turned rapidly away from Liam, needing to focus on anything but how something so simple as a shared piece of chocolate could turn into an enchantment.

"I'll just grab some of the guidebooks in the

room. Over dinner we can figure out an itinerary for tomorrow."

"No," he said. "Absolutely not. No plan."

She turned back to him. "No plan?" she asked, nervously. Really, for her it was like saying no life jacket as you boarded a rickety ship.

"Sunday! That's what you do all day every day. Let's be spontaneous. Let's just do whatever comes up and whatever we feel like doing. Let your hair down."

He didn't mean it literally, of course, but his eyes did go to her hair.

"Which I see you've already done," he said.

She wished she hadn't, because for a heated moment, she could imagine his hands in her hair, loosening the pins…

She bit her lip. Letting her hair down, figuratively or literally, seemed downright dangerous.

She could have easily gone back to the same restaurant—oh, how she loved the familiar—but Liam did not seem eager to go back there.

He had *not* been jealous of the attentions of the waiter, she told herself, but letting her thoughts go there showed the absurdity of allowing undisciplined ideas to invade your mind.

She deliberately flicked her hair over her shoulder.

"I'm in love with the duck-duck," she said. "Are you sure we shouldn't go back there?"

Something flickered in his face. The woman in

her liked it. The waiter *had* brought up some feelings in him.

"They'll have it other places," Liam said smoothly. "Let's avail ourselves of as many different things as possible."

She accepted another piece of chocolate from him and let the hotel door click closed behind her. She was pretty sure his gaze flicked to her as she slowly put that piece of candy in her mouth.

So they ended up in a different restaurant, still quaint and charming, history oozing out of its thick stone walls and black-timbered roof.

The meal was exquisite. And breathtakingly expensive.

Still, when it was over, she asked the waiter for the bill.

"What are you doing?" Liam asked, astonished.

"I'm paying."

"What? No, you're not."

"I am, Liam."

"But why?" he sputtered.

"Because I'm celebrating our plus-one-iversary. And I wanted to give you something I bet you never get."

Liam stared at Molly.

It was easy to stare at her with her hair down. It was like catching a glimpse of a secret side that was mind-blowingly different from his buttoned-up assistant.

It was more like *his* Sunday that she was one hundred percent correct.

This was what he did not get, ever: someone else picking up the tab. There was an expectation, always, and particularly with women, that since he was wealthy beyond what people could imagine, he *should* pay.

He remembered her eyes sparking with tears outside the Parliament Building, and he was stunned to feel some kind of that same raw emotion clawing at him.

How had she found her way, unerringly, to his vulnerability, his weariness of people's expectations of him?

"Are you okay?" she asked with a frown.

"Yeah." He passed his hand over his eyes. "You were right," he said. "It's totally unexpected. And you were right. It never happens to me."

"I don't want you to feel used," she said, gently.

"I would never feel that from you."

"But you have felt it."

Molly. Maybe this was part of why she had become the world's best assistant. She read things. She picked up on things others did not. She was deeply, and terrifyingly, intuitive.

She saw a vulnerability in him that no one else had ever seen.

"Oh, yeah," he said. He went to get up. It was time to go. The waiter had not returned with the bill.

"I nearly married her," he said, and somehow

he was sitting back down instead of getting up. Even though he begged himself not to say anything else, he just kept talking. "Her name was Charlotte. Weeby. I met her shortly after my parents died.

"I was feeling so unanchored. We may not have been the most lovey-dovey of families, but they were still my touchstone.

"I realize now I was looking for something. Looking so desperately that it blinded me. She seemed to be from a family very like mine. She came from my world. She fit in." He smiled; aware it might have a hint of bitterness in it. "She was good at spending money. Really good. My money. I was so crazy for her, she could have asked for the moon and I would have figured out a way to pull it out of the night sky for her.

"She was planning the wedding of the century. At some point, I might have registered it was unusual that her parents weren't kicking in anything. But I put it down to me being old-fashioned and continued paying the bills.

"The budget was pretty much unlimited, and she exceeded it. But it seemed to make her happy, so I was happy."

He stopped.

"And then?" Molly probed gently.

"A business associate warned me her family was on the very edge of financial ruin. They'd thrown her out to me like bait for a fish. And it had worked. I was completely hooked."

"I'm so sorry," she said.

"Foolish doesn't even begin to say how I felt at being duped. At *wanting* something so badly that I could overlook every single warning sign, every single red flag."

"And you've been wary ever since," she guessed quietly.

Again, that feeling, of being seen, of raw emotion clawing at his throat.

"Hence, you being my plus-one being so perfect," he said, trying for lightness of tone.

She smiled, not the least fooled. It was a smile of such tenderness that a man could lose himself in it.

"Hey, Sunday," he said, needing desperately to get back on familiar footing. "What was the building date of the parliament buildings?"

She told him the day they had started construction and the day they had finished.

"Are you going to remember everything they said on that tour?"

She nodded.

"Forever?"

"I'm afraid so."

"Is it a photographic memory?"

"If it has a name, I suppose that's what it is."

"When did you start noticing people were impressed by it?"

"Oh." She looked uncomfortable. "I mostly tried to hide it. I was accused of showing off. A lot."

He looked at her. The bill came, and she paid it, her tongue caught between her teeth as she figured out the tip.

"My abilities don't extend to math," she said, as if she had failed in some way. She passed the waiter the bill and her card.

He realized everybody had a secret pain that they carried, a disappointment, a stinging hurt.

And there was only one cure.

Scary as it was.

Each other.

CHAPTER FOURTEEN

LIAM FOUND HIMSELF wanting to drag out the evening, just to spend more time with her. Telling her about his failed relationship had made him realize how much he trusted her. It was a good feeling to trust someone. Heady.

He had the entirely inappropriate thought that he should ask her if she wanted to celebrate their plus-one-iversary by going dancing.

For an astonishing moment, he could picture her: letting go, her hair down, swaying in front of him.

What was he doing?

Being completely unprofessional, that's what. It was one thing to reward her for being the best assistant in the world with an extra day in Québec City.

Going dancing would be something else entirely. Inappropriate, a terrible breach of the employer/employee balance.

An erasing of some very important boundary between them.

As they walked back to the hotel through the enchantment of Old Québec, it seemed as if it was alive with romance. Where had all these young couples come from? So in love?

Or was he just in a frame of mind where he noticed those things whereas he had not so before?

Just as he could picture what she would look like dancing, he could suddenly picture his hand in hers, and *exactly* what that would feel like. Just as he steeled himself against that desire to take her hand, fate intervened.

She tripped over one of the uneven cobblestones.

He darted in front of her, catching her before she fell, righting her.

And there they stood, chest to chest, a delicate gorgeous blush rising up her cheeks, her amazing blue eyes wide on his, her scent tickling his nostrils, the streetlights casting a glow on her face and her lips and her hair.

“Oh,” she said. “Sorry. Clumsy.”

“It’s not you,” he assured her. “It’s the cobblestones. Romantic, but hazardous.”

Had he really called *stones* romantic? He had, but the coupling of romantic and hazardous should really provide a cautionary reminder to him that he was *not* going down that road with Sunday.

Still, he did not let go of her hand when they resumed walking. Because, he told himself, the stones *really* were hazardous and if chivalry was not dead he had an obligation to protect her.

It had nothing to do with the fact he had been one hundred percent wrong when he had foolishly thought he could imagine how her hand would feel in his.

Because how it really felt was better than anything a man could imagine. Her hand in his was a perfect fit—small, warm, soft—and yet there was unmistakable energy and strength there, too.

He let go of her hand—recognizing his own dangerous reluctance to do so—once the cobblestones were behind them. He buried his hands deep in his pockets and did not even dare to take them out to wish her a formal good night at her hotel room door.

The next morning, Molly's hair wasn't down, but it wasn't in her usual style, either. She had it in a messy bun. The change in style made him aware of how innately sexy she was, and also grateful for the fact she seemed eager to keep that part of herself under wraps.

Thankfully, Liam felt he had spent what remained of his evening acutely aware of how alone he felt, at the same time fortifying himself with a careful review of what was and was not appropriate between an employer and his employee.

They started their day at a bakery that was not in the Old City, but that was very close to their hotel and that Molly had wanted to try. Despite his saying *no itinerary*, he was pretty sure she had spent the time after he'd dropped her off looking up the must-do's of Québec City.

"Look what it's called," she said, stopping below

the sign and smiling at him as if she had prepared the best surprise in the world.

He glanced up at the sign. "Epi-Fanny," he read out loud and looked askance at her.

She laughed. "Liam! Epiphany!"

She so rarely called him by his first name. The way it made him feel when she did was an epiphany in itself.

He could feel the part of him that wanted to rigidly adhere to rules waver. And then waver some more, as he was laughing, too.

He didn't have to be uptight. He just couldn't take her hand! Still, they could just have fun. Wasn't that the idea of this extra day?

The laughter felt as if it was the foreshadowing of a perfect day, a feeling that was validated when Epi-Fanny had the most amazing display of croissants he had ever seen, including chocolate-filled ones.

They left the bakery and found Rue Saint-Louis and followed it through Porte Saint-Louis, the gate into the Upper Town of Old Québec.

Liam's concerns about what was and wasn't appropriate evaporated as they gave themselves over to exploring the twisting, hilly cobblestoned streets. They steadily made their way downward toward the Lower Town.

They went in and out of shops. They explored the Ursuline Monastery, which had been founded by a group of cloistered nuns in the 1600s. It had grown to be almost a city within the city with its churches, a school that still operated, living quarters and chapels.

In defiance of an icy wind blowing up off the St. Lawrence River, they took smiling selfies on the Promenade des Gouverneurs, the iconic copper-roofed turrets of the Fairmont le Château Frontenac soaring in the background.

From the Château, they took the steep staircases down and down again to the Lower Town and the most famous street in the Old City, the Petit-Champlain. Just off Petit-Champlain, they had French onion soup for lunch at a dark tavern, a hole in the wall, that Molly had found out was the oldest existing tavern in North America. Like so many other places, it had incredibly thick stone walls, deep sills, a roof blackened from the days the huge fireplace had worked.

"You can feel it here, can't you?" she asked with at least as much reverence as she'd had when they toured the monastery. "The crush of bodies, shouts, laughter, the drunken arguments, of so many men who would have been congregating in this city. Soldiers. Fur traders. Builders."

He could feel it, as she painted that picture. And he could *see* her so clearly. She was deep and she was sensitive, and somehow he did not want her to know how moved he was by that.

He raised an eyebrow at her. "Also the best French onion soup I've ever eaten."

She laughed, but if he had intended a light response to her serious observations to keep a comfortable distance between them, he'd miscalculated. Her laughter, and how it lit up her face and made her extraordinarily beautiful made Liam feel more connected to her, not less.

After a thorough exploration of the Lower Town, they rode the glassed-in tram that connected the upper and lower part of the Old City. Again, his sense of connection to her deepened when he realized watching her face was a complete delight as the tram emerged from its station, and a panorama unfolded one frame at a time: first the jagged, steep rooftops of the lower city, and then the wide swatch of the St. Lawrence River, a ferry chugging down it, and finally the more modern buildings that dotted the northern shore.

Molly probably would have gone down all those steps just to ride the tram again, except for the distraction of the scents coming from a gourmet popcorn shop with thrown-open windows that drew them in.

They tried samples. He, predictably, chose chocolate, even though the maple syrup and pecan was tempting. But Molly was letting her wild side out.

As they sat on a bench, he watched her happily munching on her ghost pepper and bacon flavor, noticing her hair was coming down, figuratively and literally.

But the problem was, so was his!

In the afternoon, despite legs aching from all the walking and hill climbing, Molly insisted they see the Citadelle de Québec. The National Historic

Site was located atop Cap Diamant. It had sweeping views of the Old City, dominated by the Château Frontenac.

Molly told him it was known as the Gibraltar of North America. A more somber mood came over them as they took the tour of the star-shaped fortification that enclosed 300 years of history. That early history was particularly bloody.

Finally, they stood on the windswept Plains of Abraham.

"It's hard to believe," Molly said. "It's so peaceful now."

Indeed, it was a sweeping and beautifully maintained park, where people walked the curving paved pathways with their dogs.

But from the look on Molly's face, she did not see the people walking their dogs. As in the tavern she was connecting with something else. She saw young soldiers hunched against the same cold wind that blew now, filled with the terror of young men who did not know they were part of history in the making.

The battle that occurred here shaped the future of Canada and changed the course of history for all North America.

She drew in a deep breath.

"Hey, are you okay?" he said, as she turned her face away from him.

Her shoulders were shaking.

"What's wrong?" he asked. He found himself,

despite his resolve to have a no-contact kind of day, touching her shoulder.

"I'm not sure. This ground," she said, her voice tremulous. "This beautiful place was fertilized with the blood of young men. It's still here, right below the surface."

As she had been on the Parliament steps, Molly was embarrassed by her emotion. She swiped her eyes with her sleeve. But it seemed as if the more she tried not to cry, the more unable to control it she was.

They had squeezed so much into today. He thought they had probably walked close to twenty miles.

She was exhausted, obviously. He wasn't aware how high her guards were until he saw this.

He saw that her exterior of calm control—the person who knew so much and could fix anything—protected her from a world that could be callous and hard.

Liam saw how very sensitive Molly was.

He felt as if he *saw* her. Completely.

Just as she had seen him yesterday, when she had paid for the evening meal at the restaurant.

He stepped into her, wrapped his arms around her, pulled her into his chest. He wanted her to know he accepted her exactly as she was.

Maybe even cherished this rare look into another person's soul.

As if she understood the message that needed no words, she gave herself over to him, her weight sinking against his, her sobs silent, but heaving her whole body.

He could feel the warmth coming off her as she melted into him, could feel her soft curves against his own hard lines.

It felt perfect, just as holding her hand had.

He was aware there were some things money could not buy.

A person revealing their authentic selves. Opportunities to stand in the light of someone else's trust.

Holding Molly, Liam felt he had never been more of a man than he was in that moment.

Molly had grown up in an *I'll give you something to cry about* world. She'd gotten more and more proficient at hiding her sensitivity.

So what had gotten into her? You could not *cry* in front of your boss! And yet she had done it, not once, but twice, in less than twenty-four hours!

Her outburst of emotion on the Plains of Abraham had taken her completely off guard.

But not as off guard as Liam's reaction.

With his arms wrapped solidly around her, and her nose pressed against his chest, her tears wetting his shirt, she felt the way she had felt when she had fallen asleep in his apartment. Safe.

Only this was a deeper kind of safety. Because she had revealed something about herself that she had always thought was a weakness.

And instead of feeling mocked for it—as she always had been in the past—when his arms folded around her, she felt something she was not entirely sure she had ever felt before.

Cherished.

That feeling of being cherished only deepened as they left Québec City. On board the plane, he gestured to the bedroom.

"You take it," he said.

"Oh, I can't."

But he gave her a look that brooked no argument, and she found herself in a deeply comfortable bed. Even though the linens were fresh, she was certain she could catch the aroma of him.

Lying in his bed was nearly as wonderful as being held in his embrace. Tomorrow, she told herself firmly, everything would go back to normal.

She would be back in her little apartment, back in her office where everything would be under her control again.

Where her desire to keep her love for her boss secret would not be tested over and over and over.

He woke her up gently as they approached New York. Molly sat at the airplane window watching the lights of the city, clinging to the fairy tale she had lived for just a while longer.

Then Liam was putting her in a car.

"Got your keys?" he teased.

Oh, how she wished she didn't! See? There was that greedy part that had had a taste of good things and now wanted them to go on endlessly.

Well, she had the rest of the weekend to get herself together. To marshal her resources and rebuild her walls.

She thought she had succeeded.

She had even managed to get the remainder of the false eyelashes off by the time she was at her desk Monday morning.

She had worn her dowdiest suit. She had scraped back her hair in her sternest bun. She was determined to put the magic behind her.

But her every vow disintegrated when Liam appeared at her desk.

"I've had this idea," he said.

"Yes, chief?"

"Could you be my plus-one forever?"

CHAPTER FIFTEEN

My plus-one forever. Molly felt as if she was going to melt into the earth. What was Liam saying? What was he asking? Her imagination went wild, as her heart went mad, beating so hard and fast she thought he might be able to see it.

"It wouldn't be that onerous," Liam promised.

She came back to earth with a thud. Oh. Of course, her boss was just suggesting a continuation of the arrangement they already had.

He was wrong about it not being onerous, of course. While that might be true for others, there was some complexity to Molly's situation. First of all, she was in love with her boss.

It might be just a bit *onerous* keeping that under wraps.

"It would be the odd outing that required a companion," Liam said, rushing into her silence. "For instance, the CEO of Blue Cloud and his wife have asked me to join them for dinner and an NHL playoff game next weekend. Second Chances has asked me to come to the opening of their new location.

There's a cocktail party for Hamish Peterson's birthday coming up. That kind of thing."

Just like in Québec City, all those outings would require her leaving the comfortable fortress of her office, where it was relatively easy to keep the defenses in place.

Plus, there was that thing Liam didn't know. She was a poor girl from the wrong side of the tracks.

She didn't even know which fork to use if there were options.

And he wanted her to sit across the table from some of the most successful and sophisticated people in the world and hold her own?

"Of course, I'd make sure you were compensated for the extra hours."

That confirmed that for Liam, this was strictly a business transaction.

"And you could have a clothing budget. I mean, the New York Friends of the Hudson Charity Gala is coming up at Grand Ballroom at the Manhattan Center. I know the kinds of things women wear to balls."

"A ball?" she said, weakly. *Like Cinderella?*

"It's one of the biggest events on the New York social calendar. Fundraiser. Red carpet."

To avoid looking at him, Molly opened his schedule on her computer.

"You've already asked Leanne Doherty," she said. Leanne Doherty was a pop star who could fill a stadium with tens of thousands of screaming fans. "I have it all here. Corsage already ordered—"

"I'll speak to her," he said. "She won't care."

Molly considered that. *She* was being chosen over Leanne Doherty.

It would be easy to be swept away by all this. What he was suggesting was downright dangerous. To her heart! To her composure! To her career! Deciding to say yes to this could have truly disastrous consequences to the cozy, safe life she was building for herself.

That safe, cozy life reminded her of the circumstances she was trying to leave behind, but she still had obligations. She had to try and help her brother as much as she could. How could she, in good conscience, say no to the extra money?

Molly told herself *that* was the nudge, and not the fact she could not resist the opportunity to spend more time with Liam.

At a ball, something within her sighed.

She tried, one last time, to be rational. Nothing about her life had prepared her to step into Liam's world in any capacity other than as his very competent assistant.

On the other hand, people could learn anything, couldn't they? Look at how she had taken to being his executive assistant, as if she'd been born to do this job.

How could she say no, especially given how pleadingly he was looking at her, as if she, and she alone, could save him from a horrible fate, like death by firing squad?

"I guess we could give it a try," she said, uneasily.

"I knew I could count on you, Sunday. Here."

She stared down at what he had given her. It was a gold credit card with the company name on it.

"Why don't you go see Christopher?" he suggested.

Molly felt a wave of relief. Christopher was *exactly* the person she needed to see.

Christopher greeted her like a long-lost friend. He actually hugged her.

"How was the awards dinner?" he asked. "Was the outfit perfect?"

"Except for the shoes," she said.

"There are sacrifices involved in being beautiful."

"I need your help again." She confided in him about her upcoming challenges with her boss.

"You're making my dreams come true." He stood back and gazed at her appraisingly. "Something's different. You're glowing."

"I am? I can't think why. I mean I had a trip to Québec City."

"Québec City! I love Québec City! And was Mr. Westerhouse on that trip?"

She blushed crazily. "Nothing happened."

Well, nothing and everything, and from the look on Christopher's face, he *knew*.

"Never mind," Christopher said. "I had a little crush on him myself by the time you two left here."

She laughed at that.

But then she wasn't laughing, because Christopher said, "The question is what are you going to do about it?"

"Nothing!" she said. "It's entirely inappropriate."

"Huh. One of those girls."

"What girls?"

"The ones that don't believe they can have what they want."

"Well, I can't."

"Well, why don't we give you the look of someone who can and just see what happens?"

"I don't want you to turn me into someone else," Molly said, slowly.

"It's not like that, at all. I look at it as uncovering who you really are."

"Um, about that."

"Yes?"

"You know how you heard that accent?"

"I still hear it."

"That's who I really am. I might need a little more than a few items of clothing. I don't even know what fork to use."

"Oh," Christopher sighed. "Remember that TV show a few years ago? Where gay men took a straight guy and sorted out everything from his whiskers to his wardrobe?"

"I have no idea what you're talking about."

"Oh, dear, I'm dating myself." He laughed. "True on so many levels. The whole concept of Second Chances is exactly this—like polishing a rough stone and finding a gem underneath. Not that I think you're a rough stone, exactly. But let's see what Ramone's doing. We'll start with your hair. You want to get a man's attention? Change your hair."

"I don't want to get a man's attention," Molly protested. "I just want to be presentable."

"Nonsense. What you want is to be the absolute best you can be."

She settled in Ramone's chair.

"I remember you," he said.

"You do?"

"Of course, he does," Christopher said. "Molly! You're memorable."

Ramone took her hair out of the bun and let it cascade down around her shoulders.

"I can do anything I want?" he asked.

"Well, within—"

"Anything you want," Christopher interrupted her.

Ramone put a band around her hair, took out a pair of scissors and cut it off. He held up the hank to her shocked eyes.

"Look!" he said, pleased. "Enough to donate to a wig-making charity."

And then he went to work with his scissors, and when he was done, Molly stared at herself stunned.

Her hair fell in a thick, gorgeous, healthy wave to her shoulders. She was not sure what technique he had used, but her hair swung every single time she moved. It framed her face in a way that made her feel as if she had a brand-new face.

But he wasn't done. He tut-tutted over her removed eyelashes, and carefully applied new ones. And then he got out his makeup kit and *taught* her.

"See how a line here makes your cheeks hollow out? You see how this makes your lips look fuller? You see how you can make your eyes look twice as large?"

When he was done, she stared at herself.

"And these?" Ramone said, picking up her glasses off his counter. "Belong right here." And he tossed them in his trash can!

Molly looked at her reflection. It was exactly as Christopher had promised. It was the best of her. It was the best she could be. She did look ready to accompany Liam Westerhouse anywhere!

Christopher whistled his complete satisfaction and then whisked her out of the chair into the clothing part of the boutique.

In seconds, Molly was wearing a pair of calf-length black trousers that she thought might be a little too tight.

"No, no, they show off your ass-etts," Christopher said happily. He coupled the trousers with a gorgeous tailored pale pink blouse, silk, and thankfully the shirttails drifted down over her ass-etts!

"Buttoned up like this for day, buttoned down like this, with this scarf, for night. Ta-da! And then these!" He dangled a pair of stilettos from his fingers.

"No!"

"Just try them," he wheedled.

So, she did.

"Worth any kind of pain?" he asked her.

And, of course, they were.

He helped her choose several more outfits that could go from office to evening wear. All of them had the most subtle hint of sexy to them, almost as if highlighting her ass-etts was completely accidental.

"There's going to be a ball, too," she told him. "We're going to attend the Friends of the Hudson Charity Gala."

"Oh," Christopher breathed. "I've always wanted to be someone's fairy godmother—"

He waited for her to laugh, and she did.

"And you get to be my Cinderella!"

Molly laughed again. Somehow, he was making this so much fun.

"I'll source out the perfect dress. Oh, I can't wait to start looking."

"I liked that bronze one I tried on before."

"How exciting this is! The bronze dress was perfection."

She felt herself gulp at the enormity of the challenge she was taking on by stepping into Liam's world. On the other hand, she was nothing if not an overachiever.

And she wasn't going to just be content to be Liam's plus-one. With Christopher's coaching, even if it was a charade, she planned on being the best plus-one in the world!

Taking on this new role was terrifying, and yet

there was no denying it was exciting, too. But the thing was, it was a *role*, a part she was playing: worthy companion.

And yet, somehow, being a worthy companion to Liam felt the same as being responsible for his chocolates and buying him dinner that night.

She wanted to do it, and she wanted to do it perfectly, like a secret gift to him.

But it didn't hurt her confidence one single bit that she looked so sophisticated, sexy, beautiful.

"Act as if you deserve anything you want in the whole world," Christopher advised. He looked at his watch. "Oh, closing time. Let's go have dinner. I want to know every single thing about you."

Well, maybe not everything, she thought, but still she accepted his invitation, and he began, gently and sweetly, coaching her on which fork to use.

They had the most pleasant evening together, and he walked her to the subway after.

"You own it!" he called after her.

She swished her hips playfully at him.

"Just like that!"

She wore the narrow trousers and the pink blouse into the office the next day. She applied makeup the way Ramone had showed her.

She wore the shoes!

"Hey, Sunday—" Liam came through the door as she was standing at the filing cabinet.

She turned toward him. "Morning, chief."

He stopped in his tracks. He visibly gulped.

"What have you done to your—" his eyes swept her "—your hair?" he croaked weakly.

"Oh, it's just a haircut." She owned it by giving her head the most subtle shake. Her hair cascaded over her shoulders. And then, she *owned* it walking by him to her desk and putting just the tiniest swish in her hips.

She sat at her desk.

She glanced up at him.

Bingo.

Except that Liam seemed to avoid the office after that! Or maybe she was imagining things. He did have a very busy schedule. He was around ravishingly beautiful women all the time. He wouldn't be afraid of that, would he?

The new look would be a colossal backfire if her boss started avoiding her because of it.

She insisted on meeting Liam downtown for the dinner and hockey game, as she didn't want him picking her up at her very humble house.

Christopher had coached the outfit, and she was dressed in comfortable shoes, for once, go-anywhere snug jeans, a button-down silk shirt and a jacket. Liam was standing outside the restaurant waiting when she arrived. Her awareness of him—he was gorgeous, even in a ball cap and casual slacks—was sharpened by his absence from the office this week.

She scanned his face, worried that things were changed between them, but no, there was that easy grin, as he came forward.

It faltered for just a moment as he took her in,

and her heart stopped for a moment, as he seemed to contemplate the appropriate greeting. She hoped, foolishly, of course, for even the most casual kiss on the cheek, and he seemed to be thinking about it, but instead, he put his hands in his pockets and rocked back on his heels.

"Sunday! Have you been brushing up on all things hockey?"

"I focused more on Blue Cloud."

He laughed. "Of course you did." And then he was holding open the door for her, and his hand touched the small of her back for one delicious moment as he guided her in.

She was glad for her research as she met Grant Purdue and his wife, Katherine. As it turned out, the CEO's favorite topic was his business, so any awkwardness she felt was soon erased by the fact Mr. Purdue had the single-mindedness and focus of many extremely successful people. As in Québec, she enjoyed seeing Liam in this setting, comfortable, at ease, gracious, asking all the right questions, thinking of ways to involve Katherine in the conversation.

The hockey game was loud and boisterous and Molly was soon genuinely engrossed, not so much in the game, as in Liam's response to it. Again, she was seeing a different side of Liam—so enthused about *his* team—and she loved this glimpse into yet another side of him, a kind of boyish, playful side.

As the crowds thinned in front of Madison

Square Garden, the Purdues grabbed a cab and she and Liam saw them off.

"How was that for you?" Liam asked, when they were gone.

"It was fine. I had fun, actually."

"Did you?" He was watching her closely.

"Didn't you?" she asked, startled. *What had she done wrong?*

He sighed. "I grew up with people like that. I find them very tiresome."

"Oh." She was relieved it was *them*, not *her*. "But you were so charming!"

"Was I?" His mouth quirked upward, and she felt herself blushing that she had noticed that about him, but hardly anything about their companions.

"I grew up with that," he said, quietly, and she realized she was being entrusted with a confidence. "I grew up with women who had to let you know, in the first five minutes of meeting them, that they had a Hermès purse, worth half a million dollars—"

Molly gasped. "Her purse was worth that?"

"Oh, of course, she didn't say, precisely. But when she told the little story about Grant being shocked at the price of it, you were supposed to *know*. Grant is not the kind of guy who would be shocked at the price of anything."

She couldn't help herself. She giggled. She was pretty sure it was some kind of shock, herself. "Sorry, chief, next time I'll research Hermès handbags. Half a million? Seriously?"

"Seriously."

"She brought a bag like that to a hockey game?"

"She did."

"But where was the bodyguard?"

They both chuckled over that, but then she became serious.

"You know I'm out of my league, don't you?" she whispered.

"Ah, Molly," he said, "that was my world. One where people decided whether or not they liked you based on what you had, not on who you were."

She saw that Liam was not so much being critical of the Purdues as telling her something about his world, sharing a confidence with her.

"It must have been very lonely for you, growing up like that," she told him softly. "Being genuine in a world that isn't."

He smiled at her, a man who had been seen. He said, softly, "I can't tell you how refreshing I find you, Molly. How real. I was watching you watch the hockey game."

So, they'd been watching each other watch the hockey game.

It was a silly thing to do, but she'd done it once before, and she could not resist, now, even if it jeopardized everything.

She stood on her tiptoes. Her intention was to brush her lips against his cheek, just as she had before. A quick thank-you. A quick, *I see you, Liam.*

But somehow, he turned his head, at exactly the

wrong moment, or the right one, depending on how she looked at it.

And she tasted the cool softness of his lips. He didn't pull away from her. He tasted hers.

The whole world felt as if it shifted on its axis.

He pulled away from her, startled. He looked as though he might apologize, but he hesitated just long enough for her to say, "I'm going to grab a cab, Liam."

"I'll call a car."

"No, I'm fine."

And then she was dashing away from him. When she glanced over her shoulder, for a moment it looked as if he would follow.

Instead, his expression pensive, he watched from a safe distance as she got in the cab and it pulled away.

Over the next while, she joined Liam for half a dozen small engagements: cocktails with associates, an opening for one client, and a product launch for another, a lunch program charity event.

At first, she was worried questions about her were bound to be asked, not just by the new people that she was meeting but by Liam.

But she quickly found that most people, like Mr. Purdue, found the topic of themselves quite fascinating, and she became adept at deflecting curiosity about herself.

With Liam it was harder, because he was genuinely interested, so she developed a strategy of answering his questions with anecdotes that usually involved books.

Where was she from? A small town in Louisiana that had the *best* library. And then, without naming the town or its dreary circumstances, she'd described the first book series she ever read, *Freddy the Pig.* She had tossed in a full description of Mrs. Deverille and he would seem enchanted, and unaware she had really told him nothing at all.

Had she had a pet growing up? Of course she hadn't had a pet! The family could barely feed themselves. But she had told Liam only about a book, *Because of Winn-Dixie*, that was almost as good as having a pet.

Did she remember who she had gone to senior prom with? Oh, she hadn't gone to senior prom (never mind no money for the dress) because she'd been reading *Wuthering Heights* at the time, and she had found Heathcliff far more fascinating than any of the boys she could have gone to prom with.

"Heathcliff, huh?" Liam had responded, and they'd both laughed.

They didn't kiss again, but it was there between them, a sizzling temptation that sharpened everything—a glance, an accidental touch of a hand, a shared laugh.

As she navigated people's questions, and all the new environments she found herself in, Molly could feel her confidence blossoming. For the first time in her life she felt a growing ease in social situations.

Of course, she had a secret weapon.

It would be easy to say it was her very own fairy godmother, Christopher. He provided her with the most dynamite wardrobe and fashion advice that any fake plus-one had ever had. Whether she said her duties would entail a hockey game or an opera, Christopher always had the perfect solution.

Christopher had taken her completely under his wing.

She didn't even know how she had longed for this her whole life until she had it.

Christopher became her friend. And her confidante.

But it wasn't Christopher's influence that was building her sense of herself. It wasn't that at all.

It was the way her boss looked at her, especially when he thought she wasn't looking. It was the surge of energy she felt when they accidentally touched. It was the sense of *knowing* him on newer and deeper levels.

It was a life tingling with potential.

With dangerous, wonderful, terrifying, amazing possibility.

CHAPTER SIXTEEN

LIAM WATCHED MOLLY against the dazzling backdrop of the Metropolitan Opera House. He was aware that ever since Québec City, a door had opened in her, and as they spent more and more time together in so many different situations, she was stepping through that open door. With a new verve and a new confidence.

It wasn't just the new haircut, the lack of eyeglasses, the way she was wearing her makeup.

It wasn't just the new wardrobe—and he wasn't sure if he was happy or sad that all those wonderfully frumpy grandmother sweaters had been dumped.

No, it was in the way she moved.

And the light in her eyes.

There was a compelling new confidence in her, and he couldn't help but notice that it seemed to grow every time she was his plus-one.

Suddenly New York seemed very much like his Québec City experience with her, though, of course, the two cities could not be more different.

Québec was quaint and enchanting. New York

was high energy, glamorous, sophisticated. And yet the sense of discovery was the same: as if he was seeing his hometown in a brand-new and exciting way now that he was exploring it with Molly.

He had been going to the Lincoln Center for the Performing Arts since he was a child. In the Lincoln Square neighborhood on the Upper West Side of Manhattan, it was a sixteen-acre property that housed over thirty indoor and outdoor facilities, and hosted five million visitors a year.

But now, attending the performance of *La Bohème* at the Metropolitan Opera House with clients, it felt as if he was seeing the utterly magnificent building for the very first time.

He cast a glance at his plus-one. He was fairly certain that was the same black dress she'd worn to the awards night, but even that looked different on her tonight than it had before because of the new way in which she carried herself.

"Those aren't the same shoes, are they?" he asked, in an aside after he'd introduced her to the clients. "Am I going to be piggybacking you home?"

"Well, I hoped," she teased him.

When he'd told her about this event, she said she'd never been to an opera before. He thought she might be bored with it, but from the first moment she was the perfect plus-one. She engaged with the couple they were with; she had—of course—done her homework on both of them. She probably had a file on her phone named *Rod and Belinda Miles*.

There was no dress code, so every style was there, from people who were casual in jeans, to people in the very best designer clothes money could buy.

And he saw Molly could hold her own against any of them! This thought that Molly could fit in anywhere was reinforced by her interaction with the clients, a lovely older couple from England.

He watched her with them. They were totally charmed. She was so genuinely interested in their lives, curious about the details of where they lived.

Rod was regaling with her a tale about a very bad pony named Henry, and then she and Belinda were commenting on the dresses other women were wearing, heads together, as if they had been best friends since high school.

They entered the theatre and found their seats and Liam was aware of loving the curiosity she brought to it. The wonder.

Of course, she had done her homework on the opera, too, and was sitting forward in her seat, with that earnest expression he had come to love.

Once the performance began, the earnestness dissipated, and Molly was absolutely entranced. Liam found himself watching her face more than the opera. During *O soave fanciulla*, the duet between the poet, Rodolfo, and seamstress, Mimi, in Act I, she was rapt, her face soft with longing as the two protagonists fell in love.

By Act IV, where Mimi succumbs to tuberculosis, Molly was crying, silently, huge tears slithering down her cheeks.

He put his arm over her shoulder and gave it a squeeze.

But somehow his arm remained there.

And then the realization struck him.

It wasn't Molly who had changed since Québec. No, her appearance might have changed, and certainly she seemed more confident, but the essence of her was unchanged. Solid, funny, sensitive, thrifty, reliable, brilliant.

It was he who had changed.

She had opened his heart in ways it had never been opened before. For the first time since Charlotte, he felt trust.

He thought back over the last few weeks.

Molly had always been smart and that shone through, still, but now some of the reserve she'd always had was retreating.

Liam had noticed the benefits of their outings with her as his plus-one were spilling over into the office.

The feeling that they *knew* each other just kept growing. They had lively discussions about so many different things.

His sense of respecting her, and seeing her completely as his equal, kept deepening. Sometimes they completed each other's sentences.

But if comfort was increasing at one level of their relationship, he was also aware tension was running on a parallel track.

An awareness of each other sizzled right below the surface.

A tension that was stoked by the little intimacies that were necessary to a successful plus-one relationship.

Him taking her hand to help her out of a car.

Or putting his hand on her back to guide her through a doorway.

The way their eyes met when someone was speaking, and the same thought occurred to them at the same time.

The opera was over. Liam helped Molly put her jacket back on, watched as she pulled her hair out from under it, and it cascaded in a rich wave around her shoulders. She looked at him and smiled, and he could still see the tears sparking in her eyes.

The truth hit him like a shock from an electrical wire. He could feel its power staggering him.

"What?" Molly, ever sensitive, asked, as he put his hand on her back and guided her out of the crush of people.

He had never been more grateful than when the couple they were with begged off, and got in a cab back to their hotel.

"You know what day it is today?" he asked Molly, as people leaving the opera flowed around them, as if they were an island in a sea.

"Day?" She cocked her head at him.

"It's another of our plus-one-iversaries. Four weeks today since you officially became my plus-one."

She laughed.

That laugh. When had it come to be the music he lived for, the sound he wanted to hear…the word blasted, shockingly, through his brain—

Forever.

The truth was, he was in love with her. He could no longer imagine a life without Molly in it.

"You can't have an anniversary every week. It derives from the Latin *annus*—"

"I love it when you talk dirty," he teased her and was rewarded with a little smack on his arm.

"Which means year, not week or month."

"Well, I happened to know that, which is why I avoided calling it an *anni*versary, and called it a plus-one-iversary instead."

This was a complete lie, of course, and she seemed to know it. Still, he thought, you could celebrate the gifts life had given you every single week. Every single day. Every single hour.

Maybe it was just the power of the opera still with him: its poignant reminder of the power of love, but also the reminder of the fragility of life.

He could have argued with her about whether or not you could have a *versary* of some sort every week, but suddenly words seemed too small to say what he wanted to say.

Instead, he kissed her. As soon as he tasted the sweetness of her lips, he knew he had waited his whole life for this moment.

And everything she was was in the way she kissed him back.

"I'm going to call Paul," he said, unsteadily, reeling from the power, the invitation, the total giving of herself in the way she kissed him back.

"I have a better idea," she said.

He had never quite heard that tone in her voice: sultry, sexy, pure feminine sensuality.

She leaned into him; her hand squeezed his arm as she stood on her tiptoes and whispered in his ear.

"My feet hurt."

"Would you please throw those shoes in the garbage?" he whispered, hoarsely.

"Oh, no," she said. "Because how else would I get you to carry me home?"

Home.

She slipped off her shoes, and he turned his back to her. The crowds had largely dispersed now, not that it mattered.

It felt as if he and Molly were all alone in the world.

She climbed onto his back. He could feel the strength in her legs as she wrapped them around his waist.

He snugged his arms around her calves, felt her own arms around his neck, the sweet crush of her curves against his back.

If he had hoped that carrying her would dispel some of the energy throbbing within him—and her—he'd totally miscalculated.

By the time he reached his building and set her on the ground, it was obvious they were both nearly on fire with need.

That thing that had been crackling in the air between them had suddenly burst into flames.

This was what happened, he thought, when you tried to ignore the warnings; the snapping and crackling of dangerous things needed to be addressed *before* it *became* something that was out of control. A plan needed to be in place before the full power of the storm struck.

He knew that. He'd been fixing things his entire life.

Too late, a voice in him whispered. Much too late now.

Because there was a place in every man where logic no longer served. There was a place in every man where nature overcame reason. There was a place in every man where the exquisite madness of the moment overcame the need to have plans and contingency plans and backup plans and projection plans.

There was a place in every man that was absolutely powerless against the forces that were enveloping him.

There was no point in fighting.

"Good evening, sir. Miss."

For some reason, it was Mike's greeting that snapped him out of the spell he'd been under. Had he really thought he could bring her home? And what? Sneak her into his bedroom like a teenage boy sneaking in his prom date?

What would Maria think?

She'd practically raised him. She would expect him to be a better man.

He expected himself to be a better man!

He could not have Molly thinking he would take advantage of his position. They talked so easily together, but this was one conversation they had not had.

He needed to broach it with her. He needed her to know he could not rush blindly into an intimate encounter with her, driven by lust.

He needed her to know he respected her, completely, and that he knew who she was. Newly confident, yes, but his old Sunday was also there, right beneath the surface. Careful. Responsible. Dependable.

He could not live with himself if he did anything to jeopardize the way she felt, not about him, but about herself.

Liam didn't feel as if he should just begin this very serious conversation that needed to happen between them out of the blue, without thinking carefully about his long-range plans.

"Mike, would you have Paul bring the car around? Molly needs a ride home."

She looked, understandably, stunned. She wouldn't look at him as she put her shoes back on. All that confidence was draining out of her like water swirling around the drain in a tub.

"Molly." There was so much to say. He needed to reassure her.

"Please don't say anything," she whispered.

"Look, I'm your employer. There's an imbalance of power. It's—"

She turned to him, her eyes flashing. "I asked you not to say anything."

Her fury was better—so much better—than the defeated look of seconds ago. And yet it also showed him the pure passion, the fieriness that was right there, below that calm surface.

He could have changed his mind, right there.

He wanted to throw rational thought to the wind, scoop her up in his arms, draw that passion from her, unleash it.

Thankfully, the car drew up before he gave into the temptation.

Did he kiss her goodnight? Wasn't that the exact question he'd hoped to avoid when he'd come up with the brilliant, superflawed idea that Molly would make the perfect plus-one?

He didn't have to make the decision, because Molly cast him a look so heated he was rather stunned to find he was still intact—not a little pile of ash—as the car pulled silently away.

He'd done the right thing.

Why did he feel so terrible?

Because she hadn't felt saved. She felt rejected.

Liam had messed up, and he knew it. He'd hurt the person he least wanted to hurt in the whole world.

Look, buddy, he told himself as he got on the elevator, feeling as lonely as he'd ever felt—and he had felt plenty lonely in his life—*you better figure out what you want. Pronto.*

He couldn't sleep. He paced his room.

He thought over that stunning discovery he'd made as he had helped her put on her jacket tonight.

It was true. Liam was head over heels in love with his plus-one. He couldn't imagine his life without Molly. It felt as if it would be a landscape bereft of joy and meaning, desolate, lonely, hopeless.

He texted her.

Somehow he had to let her know.

He opened the conversation with, Hey, hope you're home safe. Thinking of you.

She did not respond.

He could feel his whole body tensing, waiting for her to say something, anything, but the minutes ticked by, and she didn't.

Annoyed with himself, he shut off his phone.

And then threw it across the room.

He stood at the window and considered his options. No, *their* options. Had she been thinking of this, too? She was brilliant. She had to know she couldn't keep working for him under these circumstances.

He wondered what her preference would be. A transfer to another department while he courted her? On the other hand, as CEO of the company, no matter which department she worked in, he had authority over her.

Of course, he had a million connections in the

business world. If she wanted, he could put all of those at her disposal, so that she could choose a job at a different company while their courtship unfolded.

And yet, as he considered those options, he felt the emptiness, already, of not seeing her every day, of her not being a part of every decision, everything that unfolded at work.

He turned from the window, deep in thought.

He had made the right choice tonight; of that he was certain. There was, and always had been, an innocence about her.

He had not spoken one word of commitment to her, and he'd nearly taken her to his bed.

Really? What did that amount to? A tawdry office affair, leaving both of them without honor.

He needed to slow this train down.

But even as he thought that, he wondered if it wasn't too late.

CHAPTER SEVENTEEN

"AND THEN he kissed me," Molly whispered to Christopher, who had just met her for lunch.

"He kissed you or you kissed him?"

"Christopher. Kissing is kind of a mutual thing!"

"I want to know who instigated it."

"Well, he did. But I'm the one who took it entirely the wrong way."

"How can you take a kiss the wrong way?"

"Oh! I threw myself at him. I invited myself back to his place. I behaved like a completely wanton tramp."

"Stop it!" Christopher warned her sternly.

"Anyway, in front of his building he came to his senses, and he called a car and sent me home. Rejected me. And now he hasn't been at work all week."

"So, he's had a change in schedule."

"I keep his schedules!"

"You need to see this differently."

"There is no way to see it differently," Molly said, glumly. "I came on to my boss. He rejected me. It's so humiliating."

"Molly," Christopher said, gently, "he did the right thing. You know that, don't you?"

"No," she wailed, "I don't."

"In a world where honor has become an old-fashioned word, he behaved honorably."

"I'm quitting my job," she said. "I can't face him."

"No, you are not quitting your job," Christopher said. "And yes, you can face him. Don't you dare back up. Don't you dare go back into hiding. You go after what you want."

"But I want him," she whispered.

"Exactly."

"And he doesn't want me."

Christopher snorted. "Not wanting you and behaving honorably are two entirely different things."

Molly contemplated that. Could she interpret Liam's behavior as chivalrous, rather than rejection? It was true—she had seen, over and over again—that he had qualities of honor and decency.

"Christopher," she said, slowly, "are you suggesting it's my turn to take charge? To let Liam know he's not the boss in all areas, and he's not going to call the shots?"

"See? What a bright girl you are!"

"He hasn't cancelled the gala," she said, pensively. "I could make *my* intentions known."

Christopher gave her an approving grin. "We need to change directions with the dress."

"But I love that bronze dress."

"Well, yes, it's very pretty, in a kind of princess-style way, but you don't want the gown of an innocent young girl all starry-eyed to be at the ball. You want the dress of a mature woman who knows exactly what she wants and how to get it. A dress a man, no matter how formidable his discipline is, is not going to be able to say no to."

"No such dress exists," she said, though she did have to admit what he was describing was exactly what she wanted.

In fact, it felt as if the ball was going to be the moment that all this plus-one stuff had been leading to all along.

"I'm sure I saw that exact dress in a window on my way here. Call in sick," he said. "We're going dress shopping."

Molly had never called in sick a day in her life. But Liam wasn't at the office anyway.

"Okay," she said.

She let Christopher guide her down Fifth Avenue. It was hard not to be intimidated. Saks, Tiffany & Co., Bergdorf Goodman, Swarovski, Harry Winston…

And then they were standing at the window, looking at *the* dress.

She could see why it had caught Christopher's attention. Floor-length, a formfitting solid mossy green overjacket, with wide lapels and three-quarter sleeves, was buttoned at the waist, but then flared open, framing an even more formfitting, floor-length underdress.

The fabric of the sleek underdress was the same

as the jacket, but only glimpses of it could be seen. Woven on top of it were embossed vines and subtly glittering flowers in an array of subtle shades—blues, darker greens, turquoises, whites.

"That is the most stunning dress I've ever seen," she breathed.

"Exactly," Christopher said.

She gulped as she looked up at the name on the store. Even in the sea of exclusivity that was Fifth Avenue, that name stood out.

"I can't afford anything in here," she told Christopher, balking as he held open the door.

"Nonsense. You have a clothing budget."

This was true. In fact, Liam had specifically mentioned this event when he'd given her that credit card for clothing purchases.

But somehow she didn't want Liam paying for the dress whose sole purpose was to overcome his reluctance and seduce him.

She went through the door Christopher held open. She looked around. She felt sick. This was not the kind of place she belonged. She turned to leave.

Christopher's hand stopped her.

"You walk in here as if you own the place," he told her quietly. "You walk in here a woman one hundred percent worthy of anything they have. Because you are."

She realized there was an underlying message here. It wasn't just about being worthy of the dress.

It was about being worthy of Liam.

It was about leaving her insecurities behind her.

As it turned out, of course Christopher knew everyone in the clothing business in New York.

She found herself being ushered into the fitting room as if shc was an old friend of high standing.

She looked at the dress. A price tag was ever so subtly tucked in the sleeve. She should have been aghast.

But to her, it was more than apparent the dress was worth every penny.

"No underwear!" Christopher called.

She gulped. Of course that was true. A dress that clung like this one left no room for lines and bunched-up underwear.

Moments later, she stepped into the dress, sliding it up over her naked skin.

She was pretty sure she had never felt anything quite as sensual as the silk. She reached back. There was a nearly invisible zipper that went from below the small of her back all the way up. As she pulled it, the dress molded to her as though it had been painted on.

Christopher had to help her with the last few inches of it and with each inch that the zipper moved up, the dress became…more.

More beautiful. More fitted. More sensual.

They stepped out into the multimirrored foyer of the change area. The dress was extraordinary. The simplicity of the cut offset the embossing, which caught the light and sparked as if fire was hidden within the fabric. The dress was held up by the thinnest of spaghetti straps at her shoulders.

Oddly, she did not feel at all like a shy girl from the sticks. She felt as if the dress had been made to bring out the woman in her.

Christopher drew in his breath. "Oh, my."

He walked around her, tucking and pulling and then sighed with absolute satisfaction. "Put on the jacket."

She did, and he buttoned it at her waist.

"Walk," he said.

She did as he asked, and the jacket flowed out and around her, floating on the air behind her, revealing only the lower part of the dress. Somehow, with the jacket, the dress was even more sexy because it whispered rather than shouted at her sensuality.

"Do you see what it does?" he asked reverently. "It hints, it compels, it begs you to take off that jacket. There's a coat check at the Grand Ballroom. You leave that jacket there. No chickening out!"

She bought the dress. And, though it was way too expensive, a beaded clutch that complemented the dress beautifully.

Within seconds of paying for her purchases, her phone pinged. She didn't even look at it. She already knew what it was.

Her credit card company warning her she'd gone

over her limit. Thankfully, she'd been spared the humiliation of having her card refused.

"Should we stop at Tiffany's?" Christopher asked. "A little diamond choker?"

"I can't even afford groceries for the next month, never mind a diamond choker."

"Worth it," he said.

"Worth it," she agreed. But inside, reality was setting in. She was going to have to call Donnie's lawyer, and say she couldn't make a payment this month.

The dress in the bag straightened her spine, though.

It was okay, she told herself firmly, to put her wants ahead of those of others for once in her life. It was okay for her to have a life!

It was worth every single penny she had spent on that dress—and the missed payment to the lawyer—when she saw the look on Liam's face.

She hadn't seen him for just over a week, since last Friday's fiasco. At Christopher's insistence, he had helped her get ready at Second Chances, which was closed for the day.

Ramone had stayed late, too, and he upswept her hair, sewing a single gardenia into the sophisticated chignon he created. He did her makeup.

Then, Christopher insisted on helping her into the dress. He stood back admiring her when he was done.

"Don't cry!" she implored him.

"What kind of fairy godmother doesn't cry?"

"But if you cry, I cry..."

"Don't you dare! The makeup." He crooked his elbow and they walked together out to the front lobby of the store.

"I'll give you a few pointers while we wait," Christopher said. "So in a dress like that you walk like this."

She burst out laughing as her tall, somewhat bulky, friend walked delicately through the lobby.

"What are you laughing at? Are you missing the smoking sensuality? You do it."

Playfully, she followed his advice, adding a lot more drama than was necessary. But Christopher approved of the drama.

The odd thing was, she didn't really feel as if she was pretending; she felt as if a secret side of herself was rushing to the surface, demanding to be seen after being kept in hiding for so long.

"He's here," Christopher hissed at her, as they watched Liam's long, sleek black limo—not Liam's usual private car—draw up to the curb in front of the building.

"Okay," she said, "I'm ready, I'll go out—"

"You most certainly will not go out!" Christopher said, as if he was a protective father vetting his daughter's prom date. "You will wait right there. Mr. Westerhouse will come in for you."

Christopher positioned her in the front lobby, as if he was the maid of honor getting the bride ready at the altar. He fussed for one last second over the fall of the coat and the dress.

Liam came through the front door. Molly's awareness of him was even sharper for not having seen him for a week.

Her world shrank down to one thing. Him.

CHAPTER EIGHTEEN

LIAM WAS DRESSED FORMALLY, in a three-piece black tuxedo, the streamlined jacket closed with covered buttons. Below the bowtie, the deeper V, typical of a tux jacket, showed off the immaculate, brilliant white of a tailored shirt. The ensemble was completed with highly polished black dress shoes.

"Oh, my," Cristopher said under his breath.

Indeed, Molly thought, dressed like that and with those chiseled good looks, Liam looked like James Bond.

He'd even managed to tame his hair tonight, and it added to his look of intense sophistication, a man who would be utterly composed in any situation.

And yet, when his eyes fell on her, he did not look composed. At all.

He paused for a moment, taking her in, and then, regaining himself quickly, he crossed the floor to her, gazed down at her with the most beautiful expression she had ever seen.

Utter and totally unveiled longing.

"Molly," he said, his voice hoarse, "you look absolutely ravishing."

"Thank you," she said, and felt the deep certainty of a woman coming into herself. And not because of a dress, either. But because she knew what she wanted.

"I want to apologize for the other night. I think I may have given you the wrong impression," he said, softly.

The old Molly would have wondered if he meant he had pulled back because their feelings for each other were so different.

But the new Molly could see the truth in the way he was looking at her.

"No worries," she said. "Let's not talk about it this instant."

There. Who was in charge now?

He cocked his head at her, as he considered this new set of rules, beginning with her deciding the direction of the conversation. A little smile tickled his lips.

As if he *approved.*

"Here," he said, and put something in her hands.

She glanced down at the long, narrow velvet Tiffany box, and slowly opened the cover.

It was a diamond choker.

Her eyes flew to his.

"A little bird told me," he said, and he slipped the choker from its box, and she turned her back to him, felt the caress of his hand on her naked skin as he fastened the choker. That caress solidified her sense of being a woman, of being the one who could set what happened next in motion.

She caught Christopher's eye. He was smiling.

Own it, he mouthed.

Liam escorted her outside, waved off the chauffeur and opened the door for her himself. She had never been in a limo before.

They soon joined a long line of limos in front of the Manhattan Center. She tried not to press her nose against the window, but she was so curious about who was getting out of the cars.

One by one, those cars disgorged the elite of New York City onto the red carpet. Anybody who was anybody—actors, musicians, writers, athletes, business people—was here tonight.

Throngs of people, cell phones out, were piled deep on either side of the velvet cords and the army of security guards that held them back.

There was a formula for arriving: the car stopped, each couple went up the red carpet, sometimes stopping to greet fans. Then they paused at the top of it, smiled and waved, answered a few shouted questions from the assembled paparazzi and then went into the building.

"You know what I'm figuring out?" Molly said, as they sat in their car without moving for fifteen minutes. "Being famous makes everything take a long time."

Liam laughed.

Molly said, "Guess who just got out of the car in front of us? Mickey O'Donnelly."

"Be prepared for a really long wait then, because there's nothing that man likes more than attention."

Molly looked at Liam with surprise. He rarely said anything bad about anyone, that confidence he'd shared with her about the Purdues being the only exception she could think of.

But he was right. Careless of the cars lined up behind them, Mickey, star of a new action mini-series, greeted dozens of fans and then proceeded to hold court on the front stairs, shamelessly posing for photos, utterly ignoring the woman he was with.

But Molly was thankful for the attention he garnered. In fact, she was grateful for the whole A-list, because Liam, thankfully, barely rated in this crowd.

She was right. The frenzied paparazzi calmed as she and Liam made their way to the front entrance of the Manhattan Center. She was so grateful for those last-minute instructions on how to walk, Christopher's mouthed *own it*.

They turned at the top, and she remembered Christopher's advice. Liam's hand resting lightly on her waist gave her a boost of confidence.

"Who's your lady friend, Mr. Westerhouse?" a single voice called.

For the first time since she'd accepted this invitation, a shiver of apprehension went through her. She had wanted to draw Liam's attention tonight, and in fact she had pursued that goal with a certain singleness of focus that had excluded thoughts about how unwelcome the attention of strangers would be. She certainly didn't want the press interested enough in her to start looking for more info.

She answered. "My name is Sunday."

She could feel Liam's eyes on her, but she didn't look at him. She didn't want to see the question in them.

"Sunday?"

"Just Sunday," she said.

"Oh, a one-name thing like you think you're like Cher or Madonna."

The remark was faintly cutting, and she realized how hard a shell celebrities must have to develop. However, she thought the slight sting—and the note of dismissal that went with it—were well worth it to keep her anonymity.

She remembered Christopher's instructions, and taking a deep breath, she allowed Liam to help her out of the jacket at the coat check. There was no missing the light in his eyes sparking deeper as he took in the full, no longer subtle, sensuality of her dress.

But she had already determined the dress was not what was making her feel sensual. It was *him*. But more, it was herself, and a desire to explore the almost mystical compulsion she was feeling to have Liam know all of her.

As much as she had always dreamed of a ball, she suddenly wished them away from here. To some place quiet, and private, where they could discover, fully, the sizzling mysteries leaping in the air around them.

On the other hand, what if she was reading this all wrong? What if Liam turned her away again?

She forced herself to focus on the setting, rather than her partner, and she had to try not to gawk.

"Look at the ceiling," she breathed.

Liam's lips twitched.

"What?"

"You're surrounded by some of the most famous people in the world, and it's the ceilings that get your attention?"

"Well, speaking of getting my attention, I think that lady over there might have a Hermès bag."

He laughed, as she had hoped he would, and some of her tension dissipated.

There was to be a silent auction before the ball began, and they went around and looked at the items. Liam began to introduce her to some of those people. Only a few weeks ago, Molly might have been intimidated by this, but she found the more she met people, the more at ease she felt.

Suddenly, Mickey O'Donnelly was right in front of them.

"Liam, isn't it? Westerhouse. We've met before."

"Yes, we have," Liam said, and her eyes flew to his face at the cool note there. Mickey didn't seem to notice it at all.

He turned to her and gave her the full wattage of his famous smile. He leaned in way too close to her. She could smell the booze on his breath.

"And you are?" he asked, not giving Liam a

chance to introduce her. "Besides the woman I've waited my whole life to meet?"

"I'm Sunday," she said, putting out her hand.

She was alarmed to find her whole hand enveloped in a rather large, sweaty one. Suddenly she was being yanked toward the man.

"You can be my Sunday, my Monday, my Tuesday—"

She tried to get her hand out of his. He held on tighter.

"Wednesday, Thursday…"

She was being pulled up against his massive chest.

"Let her go," Liam said.

Mickey ignored him, "Friday, Saturday…"

Suddenly Liam's hand had slipped between them and was placed firmly on Mickey's chest. When Mickey ignored Liam's second command to let her go, he followed up with a none-too-gentle shove.

Mickey let go of her hand, and she fell away from him, gasping, feeling like a fish that had escaped back into the ocean in the nick of time.

The two men faced each other.

"How dare you?" Mickey said. And then he lunged right at Liam, his head down, like a bull charging.

Liam stepped easily out of his way, but the famous actor crashed into the waiter behind them and women screamed and glasses shattered.

Mickey turned unsteadily back to Liam. His date had his arm, pleading, but he shook her off and made another run at Liam.

This time Liam, caught by the crowd, didn't side-step aside in time, and the two men went down on the ground, Mickey on top. Mickey proceeded to pummel Liam.

Maybe the ladies of the red carpet thought the answer to this unexpected turn of events was to shriek their dismay, but Molly had cut her teeth on drunken brawls. She was not going to stand by screaming or whimpering while Liam was being hurt.

She threw her clutch on the floor, took off one shoe and leapt onto Mickey's back. The poor zipper on her dress simply wasn't made for a wrestling match. She heard the back of it split, and then she felt a cool breeze in exactly the wrong place. But in the heat of the moment all she cared about was getting this horrible man off Liam. She hit him across the head with her shoe. He reeled back from the blow, shook her off him and then he rolled off Liam and got to his feet. He stared at her. Then offered a hand.

"Holy ker-schmole, you got a punch." He smiled crookedly, the smile he was famous for. "You can be my January, February, March…"

She ignored his hand, and Liam was up and offering his. She ignored that, too, reaching behind herself and trying to hold together her split dress.

In what moment of madness had she decided fashion overcame practicality and forgone the underwear?

In a flash, Liam took in her dilemma, whipped

off his jacket and crouched down beside her, wrapping it around her.

His scent clung to the jacket, and calmed her in this sea of chaos.

As Liam helped her to her feet, and handed her her purse, there were suddenly security people everywhere. Molly noted, uneasily, every single person in the ballroom now seemed focused on the kerfuffle, and every single person had a phone out.

Although it was probably the least of her fashion problems, her hair was out of its chignon. The gardenia had fallen out, and was getting trampled by the press of people.

Liam took her elbow and ushered her, limping because she only had one shoe on, through the crush of people. It seemed every single gala attendee had their phones out.

With his other hand, Liam had his own phone out, too, and was calling for a car. He, thankfully, seemed familiar with the layout of the place, and led the way to a side exit. Finally, they were out in the fresh air.

She realized she'd dropped the shoe somewhere.

"Sunday," he said, "you can't seem to keep your shoes on."

She was grateful to him for teasing her about *that* instead of the much more obvious fact that she had just shown her fanny to the most elite gathering in New York City. Even now, she could feel a breeze, finding its way through his jacket, to her backside. She should be utterly mortified, and yet looking at him, she felt herself focusing on the strong sense of connection between them.

She felt as if she could *sail* through any challenge life presented her with, as long as Liam was by her side.

He looked at her for a long time. If she hadn't seen the absolute truth in how he felt about her in his torn shirt and with bruised cheek and swollen lip—the cost of protecting her—it was right there in his eyes.

She reached up, ran her thumb gently over his bruised cheek, his swelling lip.

"Are you okay?" she asked him.

Instead of answering with words, he kissed her thumb. The jolt that went through her was as shocking as if she had touched an electrical wire. But she didn't move away from it. She left her thumb there, on the soft beautiful swell of his lip.

His tongue came out of his mouth and flicked her thumb. Who could have predicted being scorched by lightning was so fantastic?

Their limo pulled smoothly into place, and she pulled her hand away from his face. She was trembling.

And she knew it wasn't from the encounter inside, either. The chauffeur was out, holding the door open for them.

"Let's go home," he whispered, his voice hoarse with need, as he laid his forehead against hers.

"Yes," she whispered back. "Let's."

CHAPTER NINETEEN

MOLLY REMEMBERED, as they arrived at Liam's building, that she had made all the arrangements for Maria and Paul to go see their grandchildren in Minnesota this weekend.

They were no longer chaperoned. And it was no longer a charade. She and Liam were completely alone here.

Not a word had been spoken between them since they got in the car, but sometimes silence spoke louder than words, and their joined hands, his thumb making circles in her palm, made the awareness between them sizzle. And behind that awareness was need, naked and powerful.

A need to know each other on a new level, in a completely different way.

When they got off the elevator in his apartment's foyer, he looked down at her, his eyes darkened with tenderness. He slid his jacket from her, his hands skimming her shoulders, as he went. He let it drop to the floor.

"Molly, did you want…are you?"

He stopped, the most composed man in the world, completely unsure.

She took the uncertainty from him. She put one hand behind the strong column of his neck and drew his lips to her own. She nibbled delicately around the swollen part, but if he felt any pain, it did not show in the ravenous way that he met her lips with his own.

With a sigh of surrender, he lifted her right off the ground, cradled her to his chest, strode through his silent apartment to his bedroom. He set her down on her feet, and closed the door.

They stood, for a suspended moment, looking at each other, not taking in the havoc that had been wreaked on them and their clothing, but taking each other in, recognizing each other, acknowledging a hunger that would not be refused any longer.

He kissed her again, taming the ferocity of his hunger, imbuing that kiss with tender welcome, and then with growing need, and then with passion.

Molly answered him from the deepest part of her being. Every single thing she was feeling was pouring out of her and into him, as their energy surged around them, and then melded.

Without taking her lips from his, she reached for, and found, the buttons of his shirt. One by one, she freed them. He lifted his lips from hers, and took the smallest step back from her. He shrugged out of the shirt.

It seemed to her that Liam, shirtless, was a work of art, the most beautiful she had ever seen. She closed the small distance he had opened between them and touched him. His skin was warm, flawless, silky. She ran her hand over the extraordinary masculine surfaces of his mounded pectoral muscles, down the line of his taut belly. Then she trailed her lips over every inch that she had just touched with her hand.

He put a single finger under her chin and eased her lips away from his chest. His eyes locked on hers, he found what remained of the zipper in her dress, and lowered it. When he could lower it no farther, he cocked his head at her.

"Molly—" his voice was so hoarse "—you need to be sure. One hundred percent—"

She answered by putting her hands on each strap of the dress and sliding them from her shoulders, revealing inch by inch just how sure she was.

The fabric whispered down her, cool air touching her skin, even as his eyes branded it. The dress caught at her waist, and Liam moved to her, and tugged it the rest of way down.

She stood before him, completely unclothed. Peripherally she registered the rather shocking fact she felt absolutely no shyness and certainly no shame.

She felt a simple delight in herself, and her body, and the way his eyes worshipped that. She stepped into him, not so much bold, as sure. Her hands found the button on his trousers and flicked it open. And then the zipper. She slid the fabric down.

Once, she had conjectured, in a moment that had felt so entirely wanton at the time, boxers or briefs.

Black boxer briefs.

Again, the sheer beauty of his body left her feeling breathless with the need to know more, to be more, to open herself to the miracles of sensation, of completion, of exploring the ancient secrets that men and women had been compelled to discover about each other since the beginning of time.

He lifted her to him, again, skin against skin.

He laid her on his bed, skimmed off the shorts and came to the arms she held open for him. He laid himself, with exquisite control, on top of her, holding his weight off her, casual about the strength it took to do that, comfortable with it.

His lips sought hers, and he stoked the fire between them, careless of the bruising he had sustained. His tongue danced with her lips and her tongue, and then his head dropped and he anointed her with the fire of his need.

"Liam," she whispered, a plea for completion. "Liam."

And then they joined in the age-old ritual of creation that encompassed the past and celebrated the future. Molly was aware, in some deep part of herself, that *this*, this ecstatic joining of a man and a woman was where every other act of creation sprang from: every song, every piece of art, every fashion designer dreaming a dress out of nothingness, every single thing in the whole universe seemed as if it must spring from this single source, this explosion of life's longing for itself.

A man and a woman's deepest longing, one that lived within them, largely without their awareness, suddenly and deeply satiated.

Not a single word was spoken between them. What were words in the face of such immensity, in the face of having been part of the sacred dance of life?

They fell asleep in each other's arms.

CHAPTER TWENTY

LIAM WOKE UP with the light spilling in his bedroom window, just as Molly's hair was spilling across his chest. He could feel her breath, warm puddles of the life force, on his skin.

He was not sure if he had ever felt like this before.

One hundred percent a man, her protector, her companion, the other half of her soul. She awoke ever so slowly, and he watched, entranced as she stretched and sighed, and rubbed her nose, and seemed as if she might go back to sleep.

And then her eyes flew open, and she took him in.

A man could live forever wanting what she gave him in that sweet smile of welcome. He had the most delicious sense of being seen, completely.

They made love again.

This time without ferocity or frenzy, a slow unfolding, a delight of discovery. And then they were in the shower together, that lovely, playful intimacy snapping and crackling in the air between them.

Wrapped in thick robes, they finally made their way to the kitchen.

"Waffles?" he asked her after he'd made coffee. He couldn't stop sneaking looks at her. Molly, with wet hair, wrapped in a housecoat, sipping coffee.

It felt so wonderfully and amazingly intimate, the kind of simple moment a man wanted to capture.

"You don't know how to make waffles," she teased him.

"The toaster kind!"

They were laughing. It wasn't that funny, but pure delight was shimmering in the air between them, looking for ordinary things to attach itself to, so it could express its joy.

It occurred to him that he needed to tell her. She couldn't work for him anymore. They'd have to make some choices together about how to move forward. It never seemed as if there was an imbalance of power between them, but it was there, nonetheless.

Technically, he was her boss.

Still, he didn't want to move away from the lightness in the air between them by introducing other elements.

Not yet. He would go with that feeling he was having, of everything being all right. That nothing could go wrong with his world.

Not now.

"Actually," he said, "Maria has the waffle maker that she brought from the old country. It's one of the first things I ever fixed for her, and it still needs constant attention. Worth it though. Should I try it? Do you have a waffle recipe stored in that prodigious mind of yours?"

She looked thoughtful. "I don't. But who needs a mind like mine, when we have the internet? It's making me redundant. I'll just go grab my phone and we'll find a recipe."

She was gone a very long time.

When she came back, there was a look on her face that struck pure fear into him.

Just moments ago, he had thought nothing could go wrong with his world. Had that been like throwing a challenge before the gods?

"Molly? What is it?"

She sank into the kitchen chair. He saw she had his phone, too. She pushed it across the table to him.

"It's gone viral," she said.

Puzzled, Liam picked up his phone. He was shocked by the number of messages on there. Hesitating, he opened one.

There it all was, captured forever.

No wonder she looked so distressed! Her dress ripping open not just in front of the attendees, but now, thanks to all the social media platforms, in front of the whole world.

"Molly, it'll die down. Someday, you'll think it's funny."

"You don't understand, Liam. They're asking questions about me. They want to know who the mystery woman Mickey O'Donnelly and Liam Westerhouse were fighting over."

"So?" he said.

Her voice was very small.

"There's something I haven't told you."

It came out, slowly, her voice cracking with shame. A father losing his job and his pride and abandoning Molly, her brother and her mother to descend into despair and desperation. The brother who was going to fix it all, and instead carried them further into the pit of poverty and addiction. Her brother was in some kind of serious trouble with the law.

"I ran away from it all," she told Liam, "when I came to New York. I never told you, at first, because what boss needs to know his employee's sordid past? And then…after I started being your plus-one, it just felt as if it would blow it all up, if I told you. As if you wouldn't be able to put distance between us fast enough.

"I was so happy. I didn't want to risk the longest streak of happiness I'd ever had. Donnie, my brother, has been charged with a crime," she finished. "That's what's going to come out."

Liam stared at her, stunned.

How could she not know none of that would have mattered to him?

What mattered was that she hadn't told him. She hadn't trusted him. Even now, she was telling him because she was afraid the media would get to it first, not because she wanted to.

While he had given her every single thing he was, she had thought…what? That he was such a superficial snob that where she came from would change the way he thought about her?

In that moment, he felt two extraordinary sensations; side by side. The first was wanting to comfort her, to take her pain from her, to let her know it was okay.

But the second was the stronger of the emotions, and it won. It was a feeling of complete betrayal.

And of being fooled in some way that made him feel he also couldn't trust himself.

Because he had thought Molly, with all her wonder, was the most authentic person in the entire world.

Which, he reminded himself, was really his pattern, wasn't it? Choosing women who were very good at keeping things from him?

He thought now of how she had answered so many of his questions. He didn't really know her, at all. What he knew was which books had been present during the major events of her life. At the time, he'd thought it was adorable. He'd asked after her family, and there had been mention of a brother.

Think Huckleberry Finn, she'd said.

Now, it turned out, Huckleberry Finn with a dark side. *Molly* with a dark side, a side that was quite willing to be deceptive.

It made it hurt even worse that he had been so sure about Molly, so utterly convinced that she was the one he could spend forever with.

Now, his whole sense of what was possible was shimmering before him, an oasis in a desert, shimmering before a blistering sun.

Disappearing.

Just a mirage, after all. Just the charade it had always been.

CHAPTER TWENTY-ONE

MOLLY SAT SILENTLY as the car Liam had ordered for her whisked her through the streets of New York. She was trying very hard not to cry.

In the end, they had not had waffles. She had said she thought she should go, and part of her had hoped Liam would try to stop her.

Would tell her, no, everything was going to be okay.

Instead, she recalled the look on his face with a deep shudder. And felt completely shattered, the antithesis of how she had felt when she had woken up in his arms this morning.

Her whole body had still been vibrating from what had transpired between them. She had realized she had never in her entire life felt like this: so alive that she could feel her life energy coursing through her.

So alive that she could feel the air on her naked skin, smell the tang of Liam in the air, hear every single sound that came through those open patio doors.

After they had made love, she had been in a heightened state of awareness, as she took in *ev-*

erything about him. She took in the broadness of his shoulders, the beautiful expanse of his flawless skin, stretched silkily over smooth, hard muscle.

His hair was rumpled, the way she liked it best of all, and she couldn't resist reaching out and touching it, again and again.

But then that moment, when she had gone in search of her phone and found it. Found both of them, actually, their screens blinking away with incoming messages.

Her breath had stopped in her body, as she opened her phone.

Text messages. From Christopher. From people at the office that she barely knew.

From her mother.

The ones from Christopher seemed like the safest bet. She opened them.

Omg, girlfriend, what happened?

And then he'd sent her a link. After link. After link.

She and Liam and Mickey were going viral. All of it. Including her dress splitting open. Her backside was going viral.

But the worst part was the conjecture.

Who was the mystery woman these two men were fighting over?

But, as was the way with her life, just when she thought it was the worst part, no, it could get worse yet.

Because this was the part she had not revealed

to Liam. She'd opened the texts from her mother, almost hoping that the abundance of them meant there was some new family catastrophe unfolding.

But no, her mother, who lived on the internet late at night, was also sending her clips from the night before.

Only hers were captioned quite differently from Christopher's, and it was obvious as the messages went on that she'd had more and more to drink.

Your name is Sunday, now? Like what, you're ashamed of us?

You've been holding out on me. Dating one of the world's richest men?

How'd that happen? Like Pretty Woman*?*

You're living that life, and you couldn't help us out with the lawyer this month?

You haven't asked him for a loan to help your brother?

I googled that bobble you're wearing. It's worth fifteen grand. If you pawn it, it would go a long way.

Everybody wants to know who you are. I wonder how your sugar daddy would feel if he knew you're just pond scum?

Trust Molly to notice her mother had misspelled bauble! Still, she had known then she couldn't wait. She had to tell Liam right away. She couldn't ignore her mother's threats any more than you could ignore a venomous snake.

She'd been aware, as she made her way back out to the kitchen, that this was exactly the problem with allowing yourself to be ruled by emotion, by letting yourself believe in dreams, by *owning* it, as Christopher had insisted she do.

The problem was, she hadn't owned all of it.

Now, the whole world was going to be trying to find out who the mystery woman was. Her mother did not appear to be above blackmailing her with her secrets about her family.

This was the part Molly, who had thought through everything her entire life, had—blinded by love and dreams—not thought through.

That *who* she really was could hurt him, and damage the reputation of the company. Of course, she should have told him sooner.

But she had wanted it not to matter, even as she knew all along it did.

As Liam had become more and more open with her, she had become more and more secretive with him. There was an aspect to *pretending* to belong in his world that had been very freeing.

It was like she had believed, by putting on pretty clothes and being exposed to Liam's world—private jets, travel, culture—she could leave behind that little girl who had hidden out in the library to get away from the chaos of her family life.

She had convinced herself that confiding in your boss about your personal life—especially your past personal life—would be completely inappropriate.

Sometimes, though, accompanying him, sitting with some of the most successful people in the world, hadn't she been struck by the utterly terrifying thought: *What if they knew?*

Wasn't that why she'd given the one-name response to the inquiry tonight?

She'd made the biggest mistake of all.

For a moment in time, she'd *believed* Christopher when he had told her she could have anything she wanted.

She couldn't.

She had felt that acutely when she had seen the look on Liam's face after she had told him the truth.

Wrapped in his jacket, in her torn dress, he had walked her through the lobby and to the door.

He didn't kiss her.

There was something terrifying and remote in his face as he said goodbye, opened the car door for her and put her inside.

Driving away from him, Molly understood, suddenly, the addictions that had held her family in its grip for generations, because she had wanted to turn and kiss that remote look off his face with every fiber of her being.

But she knew the one last taste could be enough to lead to a sensation—powerful, unfightable—of never being able to get enough.

Of never being able to live without him.

In the back of the car, Molly turned off her phone and she did not turn it back on. She was exhausted. She stumbled into her apartment and went directly to bed. But sleep evaded her. Finally, the tears came. She wept.

During the past few weeks, as Liam's plus-one, for the first time in her life, she had felt like maybe, just maybe, she had caught glimpses of everything she'd ever dreamed of.

A sense of being cherished.

Valued.

Safe.

But now that her past had come back to haunt her, she was in the grip of a family curse that precluded happiness. She'd foolishly ignored the lessons that her life had given her.

Believing in dreams hurt.

Hope for a different life only caused pain.

You couldn't really *ever* leave your past behind you.

But those feelings left her with a deep down sense of despondency. A hopelessness that no amount of hiding in her house, trying to soothe herself with ice cream and movies and playing games on her tablet was going to solve.

She was going to have to find a different job, and fast. She couldn't go back and face Liam. She didn't have a penny in savings thanks to her brother and that torn dress that she'd hung in her closet, despite the fact it was beyond repair.

She knew she had to pull herself together, and at lightning speed.

But the truth was, she didn't even have the strength to turn on her phone, not even as a future in homelessness loomed in front of her.

Homelessness. That went very well with the family narrative, actually.

The third day after the fiasco, there was banging on her door. Surely, not the landlord? She hadn't missed the rent yet. That inevitable event, and eviction, was a full two weeks away!

For a moment, her heart *hoped.*

Liam, come to rescue her, the maiden in distress riding away with the knight on the white charger, like the final scene in *An Officer and a Gentleman.*

How could she *still* believe such nonsense?

She went and threw open the door.

Christopher stood there.

"What? How on earth did you find me?"

"That is no way to greet your fairy godmother," he reprimanded her cheerfully. He took in her appearance—horrible—with a sympathetic glance, and marched by her.

He took in the whole apartment and sighed.

"An African violet?" he asked. "Seriously, Molly?"

"What is wrong with an African violet?"

"You might as well have a business card, *no life.*"

"I don't have a life," she wailed. The tears came as Christopher guided her to the couch.

She told him every detail of her sordid past—growing up in poverty, her father abandoning the family, them investing in the dream of Donnie only to have it crushed by his injury. And now, her once star brother might be going to jail.

"I've always been terrified of anyone finding

out," she admitted. "Especially Liam. And now, because of what happened at the gala—because I got too big for my britches—I had to tell him."

"How'd he take it?" Christopher asked, as if looking at her wasn't quite a big clue.

"He didn't say much. But the look on his face—" She sniffled. "Please tell me it's all dying down."

"Oh, not at all," Christopher said, cheerfully. "It's gaining steam. The mystery woman that Mickey O'Donnelly and Liam Westerhouse were fighting over. I *love* Mickey O'Donnelly, by the way. I may never forgive you for laying the boots to his face."

"After all I just told you, the thing you can't forgive me for is attacking Mickey?"

"Molly—" he was suddenly serious "—all that stuff you told me is about what happened to you. Stuff happens to everyone. It's not who you are."

"It's part of who you are," she said, stubbornly.

"Maybe the best part," he said to her. "The part that makes you strong and resilient."

"I somehow doubt Liam will see it that way. If the story is still gaining traction, it will reflect on him and the whole company. I'm an imposter and a charlatan and…"

"Oh, darling," Christopher said, "stop it. In time, you're going to see this as the best thing that ever happened to you."

She gawked at him.

"Molly, you can't get your sense of value from someone else, no matter who they are, not even a gorgeous someone else like Mr. Westerhouse. What interests *you*?"

"I don't have any interests!" she wailed.

"Exactly," Christopher said, sagely. "As if the African violet didn't tell me that."

"Quit disparaging Winspear!"

"Oh! You've named that dreadful thing. This has all happened in the nick of time. You were going to make that man your whole life, weren't you?"

Molly thought back over the months that she had come to work in Liam's office. She realized she already *had* made him—her work for FIX—her whole life.

"That can't work," Christopher told her. "I know your type exactly."

"What type is that?" she asked, feeling slightly defiant that Christopher thought he knew so much about her.

"The type who thinks your dreams rely on another person. First your brother, now Liam.

"The type who thinks you can earn your way to love. It's a kind of subtle neediness that will rot a relationship from the inside out. You have to bring *wholeness* to love."

"How do you know all this?" she asked him, feeling deeply the truth in every single thing he was saying.

"The school of broken hearts," he said, without any kind of self-pity. "Give me your phone."

She went and found it. When she tried to power

it up, it was completely dead. He plugged it in and asked for her password.

He scanned her messages. "Look, forty-three messages of increasing panic from your fairy godmother. Just as many from your mother. My goodness! She's perfectly awful. Ah, here we go. *Boss.* Oh, look, it's not nearly as bad as you thought. He wants to talk. Molly, you're tormenting the man."

Tongue between his teeth, he tapped in and read out loud, *"Darling, I'm going to need a bit of time. I'm not sure how long. I hope you'll wait for me. Love you forever. Molly."*

"You can't send that—"

CHAPTER TWENTY-TWO

"OF COURSE I can send it." Christopher grinned at Molly and pushed a button—very theatrically, too.

"Liam will never believe that's me! *Darling*?" she scoffed.

"He'll think it's you. What else would he think? Aliens kidnapped you and are using your phone?"

"Love you forever?" she asked, mortified.

"It's true, isn't it?"

She started to cry again. "Yes."

"Let me dig through your cupboards and find something for lunch." Christopher fussed. "When's the last time you ate? Go do something with yourself. Brush your teeth. Have a shower. You won't believe how much better you'll feel."

Though she was reluctant to take his advice, she did, and she did feel better, as she made her way back into her small kitchen to find Christopher. It even felt like a relief to have someone managing her life, instead of her doing the managing all the time, trying to keep so many balls in the air.

Christopher held up a can of tuna, accusingly. "Is this what you eat?" he asked.

"Sometimes."

"Oh, my goodness. I hope you don't open the can and stand at the sink with a fork."

Her silence was all the answer he needed.

"Good grief, Molly! How you treat yourself is how others will—"

Another knock came at her door, loud and insistent.

Molly's heart stopped. Her eyes flew to Christopher's. She only really knew two people in New York—a pathetic life, as Christopher had pointed out—so it seemed like there was a good chance it might be the other one at her door. That would be the fastest response, ever, to a text, almost as if he'd been waiting for it.

And if Christopher could find out where she lived, so could Liam. All he had to do was open her personnel file. Not even any detective work involved.

"Don't you dare run to that door," Christopher told her, setting down the unopened can of tuna. "You stay right here."

"Oh, my," she heard him say, and then two sets of footsteps crossed her living room floor. She closed her eyes. Her heart was beating way too fast.

She opened them. Her heart plummeted to the bottom of her feet.

"What are you doing here?" she asked Mickey O'Donnelly.

He dangled a shoe off his pointer finger. "Delivering the glass slipper."

Wrong prince, she thought, sadly. In what world did Mickey O'Donnelly show up at a woman's house and she was disappointed?

She folded her arms over her chest. She noticed his world-famous grin looked forced. In fact, he looked tired. She ordered herself not to feel any sympathy for him.

"How did you find me?"

He lifted a shoulder. "Private investigator."

"That's a lot of trouble to go to."

"It was important to me. I wanted you to know how sorry I am. For the way I behaved. As you probably guessed, I'd had way too much to drink. I'm a pretty decent guy when I'm sober," he said, hopefully.

"Yes," she said, "isn't everybody their best selves when they're sober?"

Mickey gave her a wounded look that she wasn't falling all over herself over his legendary charm. He cleared his throat.

"A long time ago, Liam Westerhouse dated one of the women I'd been seeing. She tossed me over for him, actually. And when that went nowhere, she wouldn't give me the time of day, after. She said Liam had showed her how a woman should *really* be treated."

How well she knew that, Molly thought.

"I guess I had a bit of a bee in my bonnet since then. So, when I saw him again, after having just blown three whole months of sobriety, I thought, *oh, I'll make a play for his girl, see how he likes it.*

"Dumb," he said, contritely, "really juvenile."

She felt a blow to her already tattered ego that Mickey had not, in fact, been blown away by her beauty the other night. She should have known other circumstances were at play.

Christopher was standing in the doorway, regarding Mickey with the funniest little smile on his face.

"Anyway, I know it's really not enough to say sorry. I mean, a drunk like me has said sorry to a million people in a million different ways. But I'm sober right now, three days in—and I'm trying to make amends."

"That's so nice." Christopher spoke up when Molly remained churlishly silent. "And I have the perfect way for you to do it."

Mickey turned and looked at him, and something flashed like fire between the two men. It was obvious to Molly, in that second, that she wasn't the only one who kept secrets, ones that felt as if they would be absolutely life-shattering if they were revealed.

"We were about to go for lunch," Christopher said smoothly. "Weren't we, Molly?"

She nodded mutely.

"You can buy," Christopher told Mickey.

Over the next few days, Molly found herself being relegated to plus-one again as she accompanied Christopher and Mickey, Mickey highly disguised behind a ball cap and oversize sunglasses.

The man, America's heartthrob, was hiding a secret that he thought could destroy his career.

But what Molly could clearly see was that keeping the secret was destroying him. And wasn't that exactly what her secret had been doing, too?

She realized she truly loved Liam, but how could she ever know if he'd truly loved her, when she'd never given him a chance to know who she really was?

She had hidden her whole life. In the library, in books, even in coming to New York, she'd been hoping to outdistance what she came from.

But now she saw there was only one answer.

It was so obvious to her that Mickey needed to come out.

And so did she.

Liam glared at the stack of crumpled chocolate wrappers on his desk. He loved chocolate. Why did it all taste like dust?

He went out to the outer office.

His new assistant, Destiny or Deirdrehe, couldn't seem to remember to save his life—looked terrified. Why was she terrified of him? He was a reasonable man.

"Did you find out where the hotel in Québec City got that chocolate from?"

"I called them, Mr. Westerhouse."

He didn't ask her not to call him that, because what if she started calling him *chief* or *boss* like Molly had?

Molly, who he missed more, not less, every single day that passed.

He'd swallowed his wounded pride after she'd left his place that morning. He'd seen he was really making it all about him.

What about her? What about that poor kid who'd grown up like that, who'd found refuge in quiet libraries and in the brilliance of her own mind? He'd texted her. He'd said they needed to talk. Actually, he'd texted her several times.

And been ignored.

And then, finally, that grating, un-Mollylike message.

Darling, I'm going to need a bit of time. I'm not sure how long. I hope you'll wait for me. Love you forever. Molly.

Darling? Wait for me? Love you forever?

But, that clear message: Don't call me, I'll call you. Now, if he pursued her, would he be stepping all over a clearly set boundary?

Was he still her boss, which would only make it worse if he bulldozed through the boundary she had set? She hadn't come to work. And she hadn't said she was quitting either.

He *hated* this. He hated his life not being in order. He hated not knowing what was coming next.

It felt like Sunday's biggest betrayal, not that she had withheld the truth from him, but that she had now abandoned him, as if he had somehow been the one who'd disappointed her.

And maybe he had. Okay, she hadn't revealed much—make that anything—about herself, but had he asked? Had he shown interest in her beyond being ecstatic about someone who kept his life in order?

Now, without her, he recognized just how much order she had brought to his life and on how many levels. Because now it was as if it was falling to pieces in every possible way. Every day felt like a torment. It had been six days—nearly a week since he'd had her in his bed. What was she waiting for?

"The hotel says they don't provide chocolate to guests."

"But—" He stopped. It occurred to him that the spectacular chocolate samples had started appearing in his life at about the same time Molly had appeared in his life.

"Oh," he said, "check the accounts for that trip then. It'll be listed as a business expense somewhere."

Ridiculous, of course, to use resources to track down something so petty.

But it didn't feel petty. It felt like anything that could relieve the pain he was in had to be sought out, no holds barred.

Three hours later his new assistant informed him, apologetically, as if it was her fault, that there were no records of chocolate purchases anywhere among the Québec City bills.

"You can check yourself," she said, placing copies of bills carefully down on the corner of his desk. "It's four o'clock. Can I go for the day?"

A clock-watcher. Oh, face it. He was looking for things to dislike; he was itemizing all the ways she wasn't Molly.

"Sure," he said. "Go."

He did not want to look at those bills. But he did. Reliving every bite of poutine, every tour, every single purchase. Every glorious moment had now become a torment.

His new assistant was right. There was no chocolate to be found on the bills.

He went very still. It meant Molly had purchased it herself. For him. Giving to him long before he'd known it.

Loving him, or so he might have thought. Her last text message had actually confirmed that.

Love you forever. But she needed time. How much time?

He fought down the feeling, *I can't live without her.*

He didn't even know her, he reminded himself bitterly. Liam had *trusted* her with every single thing about himself.

And she had given him nothing but the names of books.

And now she seemed to be getting on with her life. This morning, some paper had a picture of her playing Frisbee in Central Park—across the street from where he lived…what kind of new torment was that—with two men.

Oh, she looked as if she was having the time of her life. The paper claimed one of the men was Mickey O'Donnelly, of all people.

To him, that seemed like pure conjecture. The man in the baseball cap and oversize sunglasses could be anybody!

As if he didn't feel slapped down enough, why would Molly be with Mickey O'Donnelly? How was it possible their paths had crossed again?

Why would she be so quick to forgive the actor for pounding the living snot out of the guy who had come to her rescue? Her hero, really.

It occurred to Liam, stunned, that he was *jealous*. And not a benign little *oh, I wish it was me* jealousy, either.

It was fists clenched, jaw tight, smoke coming out of his ears jealousy.

Still, did it matter who it was? While he was trying to down enough chocolate to put him out of his misery, Molly Littleton, *his* Sunday, looked as if she was having the time of her life. Without him.

He heard the outer office door open. Melody or Bambi or whatever her name was must have forgotten something.

Or worse, someone was coming to see him, and she was not there to redirect them. Away from him.

Away from his obvious misery.

Away from the fact he was way off his game.

The new assistant was *not* working out. People

couldn't just drop in and see him. Molly had known that intuitively.

Molly.

And there she was, standing in the doorway of his office, looking just like *his* Sunday, except no glasses.

But this was between them now: a night spent together; her confession of deception; his choosing not to call her; her not coming back to the office; her demanding space; her being photographed with Mickey O'Donnelly, of all people.

He hated it that his well-ordered world now felt like a confusing hot mess of emotion, and like he could never return to those days when Molly was his Sunday.

And his sun.

"What are you doing with Mickey O'Donnelly?" he blurted out.

"Hello, Liam."

Yeah, yeah, manners and all that crap. He glared at her.

She tilted her head at him. He could see something in her blue eyes that made him feel calmer than he had felt in days.

Like he'd been outrunning wild beasts in the forest and found himself inside a cottage, his back braced on the door.

The irony, of course, was that she had brought these wild beasts into his well-ordered life.

He remembered sitting on the plane with her after they'd landed in Québec City, teasing her about being a jewel thief or on America's Most Wanted.

It's always the ones you least suspect, he'd said to her.

How true that was proving to be. His reliable, ordered, dependable Sunday bringing him this absolute chaos of emotion.

"Still playing plus-one," she said.

"You're Mickey O'Donnelly's plus-one?" he rasped out.

"Not exactly. I'm not actually the one with Mickey O'Donnelly."

Liam went very still. He thought of that picture he'd seen this morning, of the three people playing on the spring green lawn of Central Park. The other man, now that he thought about it, seemed vaguely familiar to him.

"Oh," he said, his relief so stunningly intense that he thought he would cross the room and kiss her.

But suddenly, he realized, he could not.

He could not be the boss; he could not take charge. He had to let the dynamic shift between them. So he made himself stay where he was.

"You bought the chocolate," he said. It was the most ridiculous thing he could say. Not *where had she been?* Why had she done this to him? Did she know he loved her? Did she mean it when she said she would love him forever? Could she torment him like this if she knew that?

"Yes," she said, closing the door quietly behind her. "I did."

"Why?"

"I loved you," she said.

Loved? Past tense. He tried not to let his panic show.

"I loved you in secret," she said, softly. "My whole life has been about secrets. It's funny, how I sincerely thought keeping them was protecting you. And me. And the exact opposite was true."

He thought back on that moment at the gala when she'd given her name as Sunday. How he thought she was being clever.

But, looking back on it, really, shouldn't he have seen the sudden tension in her? The fear? Why could he see it so clearly now when he'd missed it entirely then?

"Can I tell you my secrets?" she asked. "All of them?"

Something in him stilled. He didn't feel betrayed that she had kept them from him. He dropped all comparison of this situation to anything that had happened to him in the past.

He saw the incredible—and fragile—gift she was holding out.

"I thought you'd never ask," he told her. And he went around his desk to her and took her hand and led her to the sofa.

Of course, she had told him all this in his kitchen that morning, but now she confided the worst of it to him.

Her mother was threatening to blackmail her.

Her mother. He digested that.

"Oh, Liam, I know it feels as if I didn't trust you. But it's worse. It's that I didn't trust myself, or life."

And why would she, he wondered, with a mother like that?

"When I came here, I made work everything. I don't even have a life. I can't bring that to you. Not only a bad past, but a boring person who doesn't even have one interesting thing in her life. Except Winspear."

"Winspear?"

"My African violet, since I'm revealing every pathetic detail."

He threw back his head and laughed. "Violet Winspear! That's so clever."

"You can't possibly know who Violet Winspear is!"

"Of course I do! My mother read romance novels voraciously, always hiding them under pillows as if they were porn. I think those little books saved my mother's life, actually."

"Mine, too," she said. "The library. The boxes of books purchased at garage sales and second-hand stores.

"But that's the problem, Liam. I can't come to you like *this*. I know everything you like. I don't even know what I like."

"You like making me happy."

"You know it's not enough, don't you?" she said, sadly. "I have to find myself, Liam. I have to go out and figure out how to make myself happy before I can come to you. I need to put myself in charge of my own adventure. Maybe take a rock-climbing course. White water rafting. Find some friends. Do some travelling. I cannot make you my whole world. In time it would destroy us both."

He thought of his mother, so much in the shadow of his father. What had she been looking for in those romance novels that she had felt she needed to hide?

"Molly," he said, slowly. "What if you don't have to take that journey to yourself alone? What if we both go?"

"I don't understand."

"I like making you happy, too. Could we both find out who we are, together? You've tried the solitary path. I've tried the solitary path. It seems we both have just gotten more and more lost. Let's be lost together. Let's see if we can find a new path together."

"I'm still not following."

"Let's discover the world and each other as if it's all Québec City, as if it's all just a great adventure waiting for us to discover it."

Tears were coming to her eyes. His beautiful, sensitive Molly. He took one teardrop on the tip of his finger and placed it on his lips.

"And I promise," he told her softly, "if you're not completely happy in thirty days, I'll completely refund your misery."

And then her arms were around him, and she

was crying against his chest, and he could feel her absolute trust in him, and his in her.

Her lips found his, and his found hers and a world that had gone gray burst into an amazing rainbow of colors.

And so it began.

It wasn't so much a courtship as a season of discovery. They explored New York together, bringing to it the same wonder they had brought to that trip to Québec. They saw Broadway shows, but also went to tiny little clubs tucked into brick walls that featured comedians and musicians and plays no one had ever heard of. They ate at five-star restaurants and from street stands, and in out-of-the-way diners. She invited him to ride the subway, and she made tuna casserole in her basement suite. They played cards after, some silly children's game that made them both laugh until they cried.

They went out with friends, and doubled with Christopher and Mickey. They took spontaneous trips.

But to him, the best was when they did nothing at all. When they strolled Central Park or took a picnic there, when they sat out on his deck with hot chocolate, when they listened to music, holding hands with their eyes shut.

It all confirmed what he already knew.

He was ready to sign up as Molly's plus-one. Forever.

He took her back to Québec City, that place where he had first fallen in love with her capacity for wonder, and where he had let her coax out his own.

He proposed to her on the ramparts of the Citadelle, in the middle of a blizzard, with the ghosts of history blowing around them.

Some might have thought it was a strange place to propose, but he had chosen it on purpose. Those ramparts, which looked down on what had become one of the most beautiful places on the planet, represented something.

They represented suffering and sacrifice and turmoil and conflict.

But they also represented the depths of human spirit rising out of challenges. When the challenges subsided, as they always did, didn't they leave in their wake beauty and strength and resilience? Didn't laughter seem sweeter and flowers seem brighter after the storms had passed?

Didn't the simplest of truths arise? That love was the survivor?

When all else had passed, love remained. Love carried light through the darkness, and it would, always, rise again, as surely as the sun rose after the night.

He knelt in that blizzard before her, and without him saying a single word, Liam knew that Molly understood.

All of it.

"Molly, will you be my wife? Will you let me love you all the days of my life? Cherish you? Protect you? Laugh with you? Create with you?"

And she said yes, her voice given to a wind that would carry these feelings—*hope, belief, love, dreams*—into the hearts of their children and their children's children, and a future her *yes* was shaping, and that would go on and on, beyond where they could ever see it.

EPILOGUE

IT WAS THE wedding of the century. Even in a city that knew no bounds when it came to purely opulent events, this one stood out.

It was as if a Royal wedding had come to New York City.

The cathedral was one of the most well-known in the city. With its soaring towers and detail work of the neo-Gothic style, it took up a full city block. All roads into it had been closed, the barricades opened up only for the long, endless line of limousines that pulled up in front of the sweeping granite steps.

The guest list included business people, icons of film, royalty, sports figures. Liam had never seen such a gathering of so many accomplished people from so many different fields where the atmosphere was so benign.

He had heard no sniping. Nothing competitive.

Everybody just seemed so genuinely happy, so enchanted by the whole idea of happily-ever-after. Even the few selected members of the paparazzi who stood outside had put away their normal jaundiced expressions and just looked as if they were embracing the possibility that fairy-tale endings could happen.

Anybody who was anybody was spending a beautiful autumn day at this wedding and the reception for twelve hundred people that would follow.

Liam glanced at Molly.

She was absolutely glowing. The stress of getting this event ready—a challenge to even her superhuman organizational skills—had fallen away. There was not a sign of the effort involved in tracking down three thousand missing pure white gardenia plants.

There was not a sign of dealing with temperamental everybody: chefs, guests, wedding party members, relatives.

Of course, it might not be the wedding that was causing all of that glow.

Liam rested his hand, lightly, on Molly's baby bump. She gave him a look that was complicated—excited, terrified, content—before she covered his hand with her own. All the activity in the church seemed to still as both of them waited to feel the baby—their baby—stir beneath their fingertips.

Christopher had so badly wanted Molly in the wedding party, and for Liam to be seated in the front in those three aisles reserved for family and the closest friends.

But, no, the baby was already three days overdue.

Their baby, Liam thought, again, with wonder.

"Olivia, if it's a girl," Molly whispered.

"No! She'll get called Olive," he whispered back. "Sunday, shouldn't we have settled this by now? Our first failing as parents. Baby born, no name."

She patted his hand reassuringly, "Maybe we'll just know when we meet him. Her."

Molly, his superorganizer, hadn't even wanted to know the gender of the baby. He hadn't even been able to persuade her by saying it would make it easier to plan the nursery. No, she insisted it was going to be a surprise, the thing she had once hated most of all.

"I don't see why you've chosen this, of all things, to be relaxed about," he groused good-naturedly.

"It's entirely your fault," she said. "Being loved has made me feel, shockingly, as if I don't have to be in control of everything."

"Huh." There was no arguing with that.

"Shhh," she said, her attention now fully on the front of the church.

The two men, Mickey and Christopher, who had become Liam and Molly's best friends in the world, both were standing at the altar now.

Ready to say yes to forever.

He thought of how chance worked in people's lives. What if Mickey had never tackled him that night? Never had a reason to find Molly after, to offer his amends, never met Christopher?

Was it just chance, he thought, sliding his beautiful wife another glance. It seemed like so much more. Coincidence didn't quite say it, either. Serendipity?

Whatever it was, sometimes, it seemed like two people were meant to be together and the universe found a way to make that happen, against all odds.

For themselves, Molly had chosen quite a different kind of wedding. Even though she'd been well aware she could have had all of this—no. They had been married on the deck of his apartment, with only a few people in attendance. Maria and Paul, of course, her mother, and her brother, Donnie, Christopher and Mickey.

The reception, in the front lobby of his building, had been like the best block party ever. The neighbors had come. The staff of the building, and of FIX. He was pretty sure even strangers had wandered in off the street and joined the revelry.

It was at his and Molly's wedding where, once again, there had been a meeting of chance, that divine collision of circumstance and coincidence.

Mickey O'Donnelly had rescued Molly's brother, Donnie. With seeming total ingratitude for the lengths that had been gone to to have his legal problems concluded with no jail time, her brother had been running, drunk and mostly undressed, through Central Park.

Had Mickey recognized a kindred spirit? Had he seen that Donnie wasn't trying to wreck his sister's big day? Had he seen, even then, the supreme talent that so often went hand in hand with supreme damage?

Had he simply been protecting Molly?

Or was it part of this thing called *amends* that he was so determined to make to the world for every bad thing he had ever done?

Whatever it was, he'd asked Donnie if he wanted a part in his latest film venture. That was two years ago. Donnie's good looks and natural charisma had done the rest. Well, and Mickey's introducing him to twelve-step programs.

In the super small world that was celebrity, it probably was not so surprising that Donnie was at this wedding with Eva La Lydia, whom Liam had overcome his dislike for when he recognized her as his own catalyst toward his destiny.

What if she'd signed that NDA?

What if Molly had never volunteered to become his plus-one? Would they have found their way, anyway? Or would she have continued to secretly send him chocolates, and would he have continued to be oblivious?

And then, of course, there was Liam's mother-in-law, sitting next to Molly looking very queen-like in her pink suit and gloves, and a little box hat with a veil over her eyes.

He'd overheard her telling someone on the church steps before they'd come in that both her children were so successful because of her firm and consistent parenting.

She had said it with a completely straight face!

But his mother-in-law really was a lesson in what could happen to people when the desperate edges were removed from their lives. When they found safety, and every day wasn't a hardscrabble fight toward survival. She was actually nice. Sometimes.

Suddenly, he felt Molly, her shoulder against his, stiffen. He could almost feel the ripple of shock that jolted through her, even though she was silent.

"What?" he whispered.

"My water just broke," she whispered back, mortified.

For a moment, he felt pure panic.

But then he remembered what a big part the universe played in everything, whether a man acknowledged that or not.

This moment, right now, had been planned since the beginning of time. The seeds that would be this baby had been sewn into Liam and Molly since the day they both had been born.

There was something about being a small part of such an immense plan that was both humbling and reassuring.

This was why Molly had wanted to sit at the back of the cathedral, instead of accepting Christopher's pleas to be in the wedding party. She had refused that invitation, just in case she had needed to make a quick exit.

Never underestimate the power of a woman's intuition, Liam thought.

He shrugged off his jacket, and wrapped it around her as she rose. It was a way tighter fit than it had been at the gala!

They edged out into the aisle. Molly was trying desperately not to attract attention.

She might have saved herself the trouble, because Christopher, mid-vow, stopped and swiveled toward them.

For a moment both he and Mickey looked as if they would abandon their places at the altar to run down the aisle and be with their beloved Molly and the child they already considered themselves uncles to.

But Liam raised a thumb to them. *It's okay, I got this, my friends.*

Christopher, never, ever afraid to be himself in the world, called, "Remember, if it's a boy, name it after me."

Ha. Christopher was not even on the short list of the pages of names Liam and Molly had been compiling.

But as it turned out, all those boy names were completely unnecessary.

Because five hours later, a baby wrapped in a pink blanket was set in Liam's arms. Looking into the squalling face of his baby girl, the hours of agony that had preceded her arrival were erased.

She was in an absolute fit of rage at being brought into the world. She had no hair, her skin was splotchy and her features were worthy of an extraterrestrial.

And Liam was not sure he had ever seen anything quite so beautiful as his daughter.

He had certainly never felt anything like the warrior rising within him, who silently vowed he would lay down his life, if the need ever arose, to protect this child.

Liam slid onto the bed beside Molly. It was really quite laughable that he thought himself any kind of a warrior after what he had just witnessed his wife go through.

Exhausted, she leaned her head against his shoulder and touched the round miracle of that cheek with her small finger.

A tiny hand escaped the blanket and caught his own finger, grasping it with astonishing strength.

The baby went very quiet. Her eyes, the color of slate, fastened on his face, and she took him in, solemnly, as if she already knew what she was in his and Molly's world.

Safe, in the very center of it.

Love made manifest.

He had been stoic throughout, calm, the perfect coach, maintaining a strong face, knowing it was the least he could do in the light of his wife's courage.

But now the enormity of the love in the room hit him, and he began to weep, silently, the tears saying what no words in the world could ever be able to say.

Molly's lips found his cheek.

"Grace," she whispered.

The name had not appeared on any of their extensive lists.

Liam thought of how he had been trying to name

that force that had guided so many lives, nudged unlikely people toward each other.

He had tried chance and coincidence and serendipity, but now he saw what it really was.

Grace, that force that hummed quietly and steadily, unacknowledged, in the background of a person's life. Grace, that powerful, invisible force guiding a man who was stumbling toward that place his heart had always longed for.

When he looked at his daughter, he could not imagine any other name belonging to her.

"Hello, Grace," he whispered, through his tears. "Welcome to this surprising, beautiful, crazy, amazing journey called love."

* * * * *

If you enjoyed this story, check out these other great reads from Cara Colter

The Prince from Her Past
Cinderella's Greek Island Temptation
Invitation to His Billion-Dollar Ball
Their Hawaiian Marriage Reunion

All available now!